ONE

MARSHAL OF
CROSS BUTTES

The yellow dust and the biting, gritty wind frayed men's tempers as they approached the uplifting rimrocks of the broad, northerly plateau. The whole wide sweep of the land lay ahead of them, a great rising curve of sunburnt grass and bare patches of grey rock that stretched as far as the eye could see. Here and there, the wind blew long ripples across the grass and under the harsh, copper sky, the ground was hard and sullen, matching the mood of the men who rode with Chuck Houston across the vast emptiness of the plain.

Once they reached the lower slopes, there was no trail; not even the wild animals used this treacherous ascent through the hills. In places it was so narrow and steep that they were forced to ride in single file, the long rocky spine of a narrow, razor-backed ridge rising sheer on their left and a precipitous drop on their right, where one wrong step meant a fall to certain death.

Hips hard against the cantle, his legs thrust out straight in the stirrups, Houston rode his mount cruelly. His eyes continually ranged ahead of him; his lips thinned back over his teeth as the breath gushed in and out of his lungs. He kept a wary eye too on the men who rode with him; knew that many of them were regretting their offer to follow him. But they had ridden too far now to turn back.

Reaching the top of the ridge, the men were all for holding up to give their mounts chance to regain their wind, but Houston would have none of it. He swung viciously in the saddle, words harsh in the hot, summer stillness that bore down on them from all sides like a physical pressure. 'Close up, there. We've only another five miles to ride and it's downgrade all the way now.'

'I don't figure why we have to ride this trail,' growled Ed Burke. 'With the guns we've got here, we could've ridden into the Lazy Y and taken Curry without any trouble.'

'Use yore head, Burke,' muttered Houston tautly. 'Curry is a big man. He could shoot half of you out of the saddle before we got halfway to the ranch. This way, he won't see us until it's too late for him to do anythin' about it.'

Houston drew himself up in the saddle. He was a raving giant of a man, huge and powerful, with thick fingers that gripped the reins tightly, knuckles standing out under the flesh, his heavy features covered by a three-day growth of beard. 'Now let's move. I want to reach the Lazy Y before the light fails.'

He swung his horse's head around with a savage gesture, turned his back on the others, as though knowing with a strange confidence that they would obey him. The flooding sunlight glinted for a moment on the star pinned to his shirt as the movement swung his jacket to one side. In the wrinkled fold set on top of the ridge, where the tall peaks moved down to touch the sides of the narrow trail that led over the lip of the ledge, there was no coolness. The sunlight, the heat refracted from the bare rocks, was caught as if in a net, magnified, and sent out from all sides to envelop them. Houston wiped the back of his hand over

Marked for Violence

Philip Lantry

A Black Horse Western

ROBERT HALE · LONDON

ISBN 0 7090 7249 X

Robert Hale Limited
Clerkenwell House
Clerkenwell Green
London EC1R 0HT

Typeset by
Derek Doyle & Associates, Liverpool.
Printed and bound in Great Britain by
Antony Rowe Limited, Wiltshire

Marked For Violence

Two range-grabbing brothers, one a town marshal and the other a crooked gambler who was willing to barter his soul for a slice of the range, ruled a town called Cross Buttes, Texas, where it all began on a blistering summer's day at high noon. Between them, these men meant to extend their hold on the territory by killing and robbing.

Into this Texas hell-town rode Slade with orders to clean it up and to push back the frontiers of violence a little further west. He lacked a badge yet was backed by the governor of the territory. For him this was a personal matter and he poked around where other men had been afraid to go. Because he became dangerous to have around, they came after him with guns. When one of the Houston brothers died in the dusty street of Cross Buttes, Chuck Houston swore he would kill Frank Slade for that.

But that was a grave mistake, for Slade proved to be a very hard man to kill . . . .

his forehead as the sweat ran down into his eyes, half blinding him. He cursed savagely to himself, let his hand fall for a moment to the butt of the Colt at his hip, then gripped the reins once more, touched rowels to his horse's heaving flanks and pushed it on, over the sharp-edged rim of the ledge, down into the abridging rib of rock which was, in this territory, the only way down from the high ridges. The men behind him rode in silence now, feeling the heat, eyes screwed into mere slits against the harsh, pouring glare of the sullen sunlight. The hot, burnt smell of the patches of sage and mesquite reached their nostrils and as they rode down into the downgrade of the twisting trail, the wind started up again and a million scouring, irritating grains of dust burned their faces, worked their way into their eyes and between flesh and clothing, chafing and itching.

Houston made for a tall, flinty rock that thrust itself up from the ground near a bend in the trail. There, he reined up, motioned the others to halt.

'Why are we stoppin' here?' asked Burke. He pushed his mount along until he had drawn level with Houston.

The big man glared at him for a moment, then pointed with his right hand. 'There's prints here, fresh marks. I'd say five or six men rode through here not more'n a couple of hours ago. Could be that he's got part of his herd staged out in the valley just over the brow of the ridge yonder, with men watching every trail through these hills. I don't want anythin' to happen that might warn him we're here.'

Chuck Houston got down from his horse and led it forward a few yards. 'They rode on over the switchback there,' he said through his teeth. 'I reckon there ain't any place they can turn aside until they reach the valley.'

'Why don't we rest up until nightfall,' suggested Clinton. 'Everybody's tired. It's been hard on the horses, ridin' that trail. Won't be easy to take him with tired men and mounts.'

Houston came back, swung up into the saddle as though giving them his answer this way. 'We're ridin' on,' he said with finality. 'Another hour and we ought to sight the ranch. Might be better for us if we knew just how many men he has scattered over the spread.'

He urged his horse ahead, riding with a loose rein so that the animal was able to pick its own way out of the thorn and brush. He was in a hurry now, unwilling for anything to reduce his hopes of an early capture. For almost a year now, Ed Curry had been one of the big stumbling blocks in the way of a complete take-over of the territory around Cross Buttes. As he rode, Houston let his thoughts go back to that day, almost fourteen months before, when he and his brother, Dan, had first set eyes on Cross Buttes. They had outridden the posse which had been on their trail for almost two weeks and been riding down from the upland plateau when they had ridden into the broad, fertile valley. Here, in the insular vastness of the Texas plains, it was almost as if the outside world of stretching desert, empty waterholes and endless mesas had never existed. They had been in no hurry as they had ridden west, through the valley and then around the low sweep of the hills, riding loosely in the saddle, studying the land, the distant mountains to the north-west, the first scattered signs of life, small isolated homesteads and the glimpses of larger ranches, herds of red-brown cattle grazing by the banks of the broad river.

This, they had thought, was a prosperous valley; the people would be wealthy and comfortable, knowing peace, not too watchful or suspicious of strangers, not expecting trouble. It was only in territory where the topsoil was thin and would not support the grass necessary for cattle to feed and fatten that the people were edgy and troublesome.

They had ridden into Cross Buttes shortly before sundown, had looked the place over during the three days which followed. It was all they had thought it would be. A thriving community, centre of a prosperous territory, with plenty of cowhands coming in to spend their wages and prospectors from the hills moving in with their hard-won gold dust, panned from the rushing streams which ran down from the summits of the Elklands and joined near the valley to form the sluggish river which ran through the grasslands. Law in Cross Buttes was vested in an aging sheriff who may have been gunfast in his younger days, but was now so slow that he had stood no chance against the man who had called him out in the darkness, a man who had shot him down on the steps of the saloon and vanished without a trace into the moonthrown shadows.

With nobody willing to stand for the post of Town Marshal, it had been a comparatively simple matter to find enough citizens to elect him to the post and since that time, things had been going their way. Dan was making good pickings in the saloons, fleecing the prospectors and cowhands who came in at regular intervals, their pockets filled with gold.

The first sign of trouble had come from Ed Curry when a bunch of his boys had started a ruckus in the saloon, accusing Dan of cheating with the cards. Chuck Houston's lips curled in a vaguely cynical sneer as he thought of that incident. Perhaps Dan had been a little slow; it was not usual for him to be found out like that. But as Town Marshal, he had stepped in before the brawl could develop into anything more. Two of the trail hands had finished inside the jail house, another had been shot in the shoulder when he had attempted to resist and when Curry had arrived in town the next morning, seeking his men, he had been forced to pay the two hundred dollars fine on the men for creating a disturbance in Cross Buttes. Since that time, Curry had gone out of his way to try to run Dan and himself out of town, had tried to talk the citizens who had elected him into this post, Wallis the banker,

9

Thoroton and Bailey, two of the more important store-keepers, to reverse their earlier decision and vote him out of office. Now had come the time of reckoning. He had thought it all out very carefully. Getting Cal Weston, one of Curry's neighbours, to put in a charge that Curry had been running some of his beef off the range and into his own herd had been a simple matter. Now he was going to take Curry in for rustling and once the other was locked inside the town jail, he would soon find a way of inflaming the passions of the mob. Weston would have started that already in the saloons and it would need very little to get the townsfolk worked up to a lynching.

Tilting back his hat-brim, he drew himself up in the saddle, threw a quick, searching glance along the undulating horizon where the hills drew close to the edges of the trail on two sides. For a little way, the trail continued up again, but soon levelled off, wound its way between two tall pillars of rock. On the other side of the narrow pass lay the valley which marked the western end of the Lazy Y.

Down in the valley, they were compelled to ride clear of their cover, but the herd which he had expected to find there was nowhere in sight. For a moment, the fact troubled him, then he pushed it out of his mind. He had enough men at his back to take care of the Lazy Y crew. But in spite of this, he dug his toes into the stirrups, shaded his eyes against the sunlight and ran his gaze along the crests of the hills near at hand, watching for the tell-tale glint of sunlight reflected from a rifle barrel, saw nothing like that and shrugged.

The trail continued on and took them presently to one of the many small, square meadows which creased the lower folds of the hills. Turning into the timber, they stayed with the cover until they came in sight of the ranch. It lay in a hollow among the crowding hills, the house and barns beside one of the small streams, a corral fenced in on one side of the dusty courtyard. They paused at the very fringe of the timber and let their horses blow, watching the open area over which they would have to ride to reach the ranch.

'Those horses outside the ranch must belong to that party we've been trailin',' muttered Burke with a faint grin.

'Could be,' Houston nodded. He eased the Colt a little in its holster with an absent movement of his right hand. 'We'll wait and see if they decide to leave.'

The smell of the day was all about them, a smell compounded of dust and dried sage and the aromatic scent of the pines at their backs. Houston built himself a smoke, lit it and inhaled deeply, turning his hard, steely gaze outward as far as he could see. His horse's shoulder muscles quivered from the exertion of the long, hard ride over the hills and its hide was shiny with sweat.

'I thought you said we'd just ride in and take him,' growled Burke savagely. 'Why sit up here waiting?'

'Because we're goin' to do things my way,' snapped Houston sharply. 'If we ride on down there now and call Curry out, he could barricade himself in that place with those men and keep us at bay for hours.'

'And if they don't show any sign of movin' on?'

'If they are Curry's men, and I don't doubt it, then they'll move on soon.'

'Could be they're movin' now,' said one of the other men. He pointed.

Houston turned his head, stared in the direction of the man's pointing finger. The door of the ranch had opened and a small group of men had come out on to the low porch. They stood talking together for several moments, then stepped down into the courtyard, climbed up into the saddle. One man only remained where he was in the open doorway and Houston recognized him at once. Ed Curry. He felt a little thrill of exultation run through him. This was going to be a lot easier than he had expected.

Moments later, the men in the courtyard touched spurs to their mounts and galloped off, lifting a cloud of grey-yellow dust which hung in the still air, hiding them from view until they emerged, further along the trail, riding up into the hills.

Houston nodded. 'That's it, boys,' he said tightly. 'Now let's go and pay a call on Mr. Curry.'

He rowelled his mount viciously, put it swiftly down the grassy slope, the rest of the posse thundering after him. The door of the ranch was shut as they rode into the court-yard, the dust kicked up by the other riders stinging the backs of their nostrils.

'Curry! We know you're in there,' he called loudly. 'Come on out. I want to talk to you.'

Almost before the words were out of his mouth, the door was pulled open and Curry stood there, a rifle in his hands, the barrel trained on Houston's chest.

'I've got nothin' to discuss with a crooked Town Marshal such as you, Houston,' he gritted. 'Now get off my land or I'll shoot you down.'

Houston grinned thinly. He leaned forward, resting his elbows on the saddle horn, but not once taking his eyes off the other's face. 'Now don't be a fool, Curry and stop treatin' me like one. There are a dozen guns trained on you this minute, so drop that rifle. Drop it, I say!'

For a moment, defiance showed on the other's bluff features. But there was evidently no alternative to obedience. The thought of action lived a moment longer in his face and his finger was hard on the trigger of the weapon. Then he lowered it reluctantly.

'All right, Houston. Speak your piece and then go. If you're here to complain about any of my men, then you're wastin' your time. I've given them orders to stay out of town until we get ourselves a decent, honest lawman there.'

Houston tightened his lips, the muscles of his jaw standing out under the skin. For a moment he was tempted to draw his gun and shoot the other down, then fought down the urge. This was neither the time nor the place for murder. His voice was flinty as he said: 'There's a man in Cross Buttes who claims you've been rustlin' his beef. Now as marshal, I figure it's up to me to go out and bring in the rustlin' varmint. That's what I'm doin'.'

'Rustlin' cattle? What in tarnation are you talkin' about now, Houston?'

'About Cal Weston's beef. I reckon you figured that you could run those steers off the range and nobody would suspect the big rancher of doin' anything as low down as that. But, by God, you made a big mistake. I'm takin' you back into town for trial.'

'Like hell you are,' snapped the other. He swung the hand holding the rifle up swiftly, lining the barrel once more on Houston. It was swinging into line when the gun in Houston's fist roared. Curry let out a wild yell and dropped the weapon on to the boards of the porch as the bullet from the smoking Colt smashed into his wrist. He stood with his left hand clasped about the other, the blood trickling down his hand and dripping off the ends of his fingers.

'Now get your bronc and saddle up,' Houston rasped. 'I don't want to have to kill you, Curry, but you're sure makin' it hard for me not to.'

'This is all a put-up job you've trumped up with Weston,' said the other thinly. 'Do you think I can't see through your little scheme, Houston? Ever since I swore I'd run you and your cheatin' brother out of town and put a straight-shooting lawman in your place, you've been tryin' to get rid of me.' He turned a little, let his scathing glance run over the faces of the men who sat behind Houston. 'I know most of you men,' he said scornfully. 'I always had you figured as decent, law-abidin' citizens of Cross Buttes. Most of you have lived there all your lives, yet you allow a gunslinger like this man to ride in and take over, and you not only fail to stop him, you aid him in his work.'

Houston's lips curled into a cynical smile as he saw the looks of vague discomfort which spread over the faces of some of the men. He could guess at what they were thinking at that moment. Curry's words had undoubtedly stung them.

'All we're doin' is askin' you to ride with us back to town,' said Calter uneasily. 'Ain't no talk of gettin' rid of you, Mister Curry. If it's Weston who's lyin' then we'll find out and you can ride back here and there'll be no harm done.'

'You're a stupid, blind fool, Calter. Who owns Cross Buttes now? You and the other townsfolk?' He shook his head, pain creasing his face. 'Houston here owns everythin' there. Him and that cheatin' brother of his.'

'One more word out of you, Curry, and I'll put another bullet into you and the next will be in your heart,' said Houston ominously. 'Now get your mount out of the corral and saddle up. Hurry!'

Curry obeyed, finally, his lips drawn flat across his teeth. He climbed up into the saddle with an obvious effort, unable to use his right hand, swayed for a moment, then gripped the reins with a tight-fisted hold with his left hand.

'That's better. Now you're showin' some sense,' sneered Houston. He thrust the Colt back into its holster. 'All right, let's ride. The sooner we get the prisoner into a cell the sooner we can wash this trail dust out of our throats.'

They rode out of the valley, up through the hills and then down into the narrow wrinkles of ground which lay on the other side. Houston rode with a feeling of inner satisfaction in his mind. Everything had gone well so far. Now a lot would depend on whether Weston did his work well in town. If he did, then Curry would be swinging from the most convenient tree by dawn and the biggest obstacle in his way would be over.

Just as the red disc of the sun touched the tops of the hills to the north, they rounded a bend in the trail and came in sight of Cross Buttes. It lay in a sprawling mass across the trail in the centre of a wide valley. Here, the hills seemed to have become pushed further back, giving an air of open spaciousness to the town. Lights were beginning to gleam yellow in the windows as they rode slowly down the dusty main street. Cross Buttes was a town which had been thrown up quickly in the hard, frontier days when the dividing line between the known and the unknown in this territory had been among these hills. Now the tide of civilisation had moved a little further west, a couple of hundred miles perhaps, but not more, unless one counted the wagon trains which had pushed on to the frontiers with California. But between Cross Buttes and the rich goldfields of that westernmost State were hundreds of miles of wild desert with a bare handful of dangerous trails criss-crossing the country.

At either end of Cross Buttes stood a large saloon, with stores and offices ranged thereafter along either side of the street. Near the middle of the street, almost directly opposite the hotel, the only double-storied building in the middle of the town, stood the sheriff's office and the jail-house. It was towards this building that Houston led his men.

Reining his mount, he gestured to Curry. 'Get down off your horse and don't try anythin' funny,' he warned. He relaxed a little, tilted back his head and stared hard at the other, his right hand hovering close to the butt of the Colt.

Curry glared at the other for a long moment, still defiant. Then he hooked one leg over the saddle and slid to the ground, resting his shoulders against his horse's flank for a moment to steady himself.

Dismounting, Houston moved towards the other, slid

the Colt from its holster and prodded the other in the small of the back none too gently with it. 'Inside,' he said harshly. 'And if you're figurin' on any of the townsfolk to help you, better think again. Weston has been spreadin' the word around town about you ridin' off some of his prime beef and in these parts, folk don't cotton on too well to rustlers.'

'You know damned well that it's a lie,' snarled the rancher. 'And once my men hear of this, they'll come ridin' into Cross Buttes and take the whole town apart, and when that happens, you'll soon find out how many of these deputies you've sworn in will stand by you.'

For just a second, the mask slipped on the marshal's features. Then it was back again, tight-lined and dangerous. 'Shut up and do as you're told,' he warned.

Curry let his gaze move around the circle of watching men, then shrugged his shoulders resignedly and walked up on to the boardwalk, through into the building with Houston close on his heels.

Locking the door of the cell, he paused outside in the narrow corridor for a moment, staring in at the other. Grinning, he said tersely: 'Guess I should apologise about the conditions here, Curry. Gets mightly hot durin' the day and cold at night. But it shouldn't be more'n a couple of weeks before the circuit judge gets here and I reckon I can promise you a quick trial.'

'If you try to hold me here on this trumped up charge, you'll never live to see it, Houston,' said Curry, speaking through tightly-clenched teeth. Something moved at the back of his deep-set eyes. 'And you know that nobody in Cross Buttes will back your play when my boys ride into town. They'll burn this place to the ground.'

Houston spread his hands wide. 'Now why get so all-fired het up about this, Curry? Somebody makes a complaint to me and I got to act on it. If I'm supposed to be the law around here I can't afford to ignore such a thing. All I did was ride out to your place and ask you to come back with me so we can sort this thing out. If Weston is lyin', then you go free. It's as simple as that.' Turning way from the other, he added: 'Mind you, Curry, I guess I should warn you that he does have some mighty strong evidence to support his claim.'

Curry's lips curled back from his teeth. In the dim light inside the cell, his face was almost in shadow. 'You know as well as I do that evidence like that can be faked. Men will swear to anythin' so long as they're paid enough.'

Houston shrugged, crushed his hat on top of his head. 'I don't want to hear any more about that.'

As he turned to move away, the prisoner considered his back for a moment and then said, his tone sharp-edged with anger and frustrated indignation: 'You got no right to hold me here, Marshal.' He deliberately stressed the last word. 'I figure there's somethin' more to this than meets the eye You've got some scheme workin' in that crooked mind of yours and—'

Houston swung back. 'I warned you before, Curry. Shut up! I don't want to hear any more of your ideas or pleas. Just sit tight and behave yourself and you'll be all right. Now I'll see the Doc about that hand of yours and get a tray of supper sent over from the saloon.'

'You can go to hell, Houston,' snarled the rancher.

Houston left the office, stepped down into the cool dimness of the evening and walked slowly along the street to the restaurant. It was a low-built adobe structure, more decrepit than most of the other buildings along that stretch of the street, but there was good, well-cooked food to be had here and he seldom went anywhere else for supper. There was a packed dirt floor and a counter that stretched along one side of the room, with the small kitchen through the wall at the back.

'The usual for me,' he said to the man at the back of the

counter, 'and you'd better send a tray in for the prisoner.'

The other's eyebrows went up. He said casually, too casually: 'Saw you ride back into town with Ed Curry, Marshal. You holdin' him for somethin'?'

'That's right.' The other nodded tersely. 'Now how about the supper?'

'Comin' right up, Marshal,' said the other hurriedly. He disappeared through the door in one corner of the room.

Houston seated himself wearily in the chair near the window where he could look out and watch the street. Outside, the night had thrown a velvet mantle over the town, hiding most of the details. Men on the opposite boardwalk were seen as vague shadows, their faces lit alternately by the light streaming from the windows, and hidden in the darkness which lay in between. The town would be seething with trouble and discontent now, he reckoned. The word would have gone around that Ed Curry had run off several hundred head of Weston's prime cattle and that Houston had taken out a posse to bring him in for questioning, and to hold him until the circuit judge arrived there for the trial. Houston had deliberately waited until this moment before making his move against Curry so that Weston could inflame the hot-headed elements among the townsfolk.

Eating his meal, Houston reflected on Curry's threat to have his men ride into town and raze the place to the ground. This bothered him although he did not want to admit it, even to himself He knew of Curry's men, knew they were all handy with a gun, fast men. And although the posse might have stood with him out there on the trail, back here in Cross Buttes. it was a very different matter.

Still, unless he had badly miscalculated, once Curry himself was swinging from the end of a rope, that would be the end of the matter. These hired gunmen owed their allegiance to Curry only so long as he was alive to give orders.

He drank down two cups of scalding black coffee to wash the trail dust out of his throat and made himself a smoke, scowling down into his cup. The trouble was he had an intuitive feeling that something was going to go wrong with this deal. What it might turn out to be, he could not guess at that moment: but it was a feeling which had been growing stronger with every passing minute.

'You got Curry locked up in the jailhouse?' asked a voice from directly above him.

Houston looked up sharply, stared into the amused, vaguely cynical eyes of his brother. Dan Houston was slim-built in contrast to his more beefy brother, his face thinned until the flesh seemed to he drawn down tightly on the bones of his cheeks. his mouth a tight, red gash, now twisted into a veiled grin. His long-fingered hands rested on the back of the other's chair and the black frock-coat he wore gave him an almost ghoulish appearance. Only when he made a slight movement before sitting down, did the coat flip back a little, to reveal the Colt strapped to his thigh. There would be a small but deadly Derringer concealed somewhere on his person, Chuck mused, ready for instant use.

'He's safely locked away,' Chuck Houston muttered. He finished his coffee with a single gulp, wiped the back of his hand across his lips. 'You're not worried overmuch about him are you?'

Dan shrugged his shoulders complacently. 'Ain't no way he can bust out of that jail without help from outside and nobody in this town is going to lift a finger to help him now.'

'You sure of that?' demanded the other, leaning forward a little as he lit the cigarette and drew the sweet smoke deeply into his lungs.

'Of course.' The other's gaze brightened slightly and then it turned ironic. 'I helped Weston spread the word around. By now, most of the men in the saloons will be gettin' free drinks and it won't be too long before they get into a lynchin' mood. Then you just play your part convincingly and Curry is finished.'

'I hope you're right.' Chuck sounded dubious. 'He's got plenty of men back at the Lazy Y and if they was to ride out here and start trouble, we'd not be able to hold 'em.'

'Stop worryin'. It's all fixed, I tell you.' Dan Houston crooked a finger in the direction of the man behind the counter, ordered coffee. He sat back in his chair, his gaze fixed on his brother. Then he turned his pinched down eyes on his cup as the coffee was placed in front of him. His grin took on a savage, ugly thinness 'Weston will do his job well. He knows what to expect if he doesn't.'

'I tell you I seen them cattle o' mine with my own eyes – and Hogarth, my foreman, saw 'em too. Weren't no mistakin' 'em. All had the scars where my brand had been changed to that of the Lazy Y.'

There were six men sitting in one corner of the saloon, with Weston leaning his shoulders against the back of his chair, pausing to let his words sink in, eyeing his companions closely from under lowered lids. He had both of his fisted hands thrust deep into the pockets of his pants. 'And for my money he's goin' to go on rustlin' cattle until he's the biggest man in the whole goshdarned territory and unless we do somethin' about it now, we won't be able to stop him mighty soon.'

'How'd you figure we might stop him?' asked one of the listeners. He sat with his eyes nearly closed. 'The marshal has him locked away in one of the cells in the jailhouse. Curry won't get out of there in a hurry and neither will anybody else get in.'

'Could be that the marshal could be made to see reason,' said Weston tightly. 'I got a feelin' he don't cotton on to Curry's action any more than we do. He won't be able to do anythin' openly. but if a bunch of us were to go on over there and force him to open up that cell and turn Curry over to us, could be he wouldn't put up much of a fight.'

'Reckon you could be right at that.' Hewitt, a tall, thin-faced, gangling man shot the rancher a sidelong glance. 'Ain't no love lost between Houston and Curry, not since there was that trouble with the marshal's brother.'

'Then why are we just sittin' here – talkin'?'

Weston held up his hand. 'Whatever happens, don't let's go off half-cocked. Curry has got friends here in Cross Buttes, influential friends and he's also got men back there on the Lazy Y ranch who might come ridin' out to bust him out of the jail. This has all got to be planned carefully. It's too open here to discuss it. I suggest we meet someplace else after midnight.'

'The old storehouse along the street,' suggested Hewitt.

'All right, the old storehouse it is,' Weston agreed. 'But make it casual. and don't attract any attention. We don't want Houston to be warned before we're ready.'

Hours ticked away. It was almost grey dawn and all of Cross Buttes seemed to be still asleep. The main street was deserted, had been that way for hours. Yet in the shadows close to one of the tumble-down buildings, near the edge of town, a man lounged, visible only when he drew deeply on his cigarette, the glowing tip winking on and off like a tiny fist beating against the dark curtain.

He stood quite still for a long while, keeping an eye on the empty street as if oblivious to everything else, the high collar of his jacket turned up against the night wind that swept along the street, blowing cold off the crests of the distant mountains. Slowly, the grey light filtered among the quiet houses, touched the street and made a veiled pattern of silver along the slatted boardwalks. Soon, it would be full daylight and Cross Buttes would begin to stir and shake itself awake. Letting the glowing butt of the cigarette fall to the dust at his feet, he ground it into the dirt with his toe, straightened, cast a final swift glance alone the street in either direction, then motioned with his right hand.

The men came out of the shadowed alleyway which ran between two of the houses and then lost itself in a maze of similar alleys in the rabbit warren away from the main street.

'Light's on in the sheriff's office,' the man grunted. He jerked a thumb along the street. 'Went on a couple of minutes ago.'

'Good,' muttered Weston. He slid the Colt up and down in its holster for a few times, then thrust it deep into leather with a final gesture. 'Let's go. I aim to give this *hombre* Curry a trial all my own, in full view of the townsfolk. Then they can stand and watch the sentence carried out if they have a mind to.' He grinned viciously.

They plodded through the cool greyness of the dawn scarcely passing a remark among themselves, strung out across the breadth of the main street. As usual, at that early hour of the morning, Cross Buttes was as still as the grave with only two yellow lights showing, that in the lawman's office and the other a little further along the street where the doctor had his surgery. Stepping up on to the boardwalk outside the sheriff's office, their footfalls sounding hollowly and loud in the clinging stillness, they paused outside the door while Weston tried the handle gently. When it gave under his touch, he threw the door open and stepped inside, jerking the gun from its holster and lining up the barrel on the burly figure of the marshal as he dozed in his chair, legs up on the wooden desk.

Heaving himself upright, pulling his legs down, Houston stared blankly at the men who came crowding into the small office, pretending not to notice the broad wink which Weston gave him, his face turned away from the others so that the rest of the men saw nothing of this.

'All right, Marshal. We know you've got that rustling varmint, Curry, in the cells. We've come to give him a proper trial. Ain't no sense hangin' around here waitin' for the circuit judge to arrive. Could be weeks yet and in that time, you'll have to let Curry go. You got no real evidence against him.'

'Now see here, boys,' Houston spread his hands flat on top of the desk in front of him. 'You can't bust in here and try to take the law into your own hands. You know that as well as anybody, Weston. There's the due process of the law to be gone through and only a duly appointed judge can pass sentence on a prisoner.'

'Marshal, you got no call to try to stop us. You know we've got plenty of evidence against Curry and you know that soon, if you still hold him, those hired killers of his will ride into town and bust him out of jail and you won't be able to stop 'em. We aim to see justice done before that happens.'

'You can't take a man out and try him yourselves,' protested Houston, 'and what proof have you got that he's been rustlin' your beef?'

'Proof enough for us,' one of the other men snarled. He made a menacing movement with his sixgun. 'Now get your keys and bring him out to us. Leave your guns behind on the desk.'

Houston hesitated for a moment, the unbuckled his gunbelt and placed it on the desk in front of him. 'You're makin' a big mistake. boys. You take Curry out and lynch him and it'll be my sworn duty to hunt you down and bring you to trial for murder.'

'You don't scare us, Houston. We know the men who elected you as Town Marshal and I figure we can get them to reverse their decision if we've got a mind to.'

Weston jerked his head towards one of the waiting men. 'I don't trust him too much.' he said sharply. 'Get his keys and bring Curry out here.'

'Sure.' The man stepped forward, took down the bunch of keys from the hook on the wall at the back of the desk. keeping a wary eye on the lawman. He went out through the door in the corner of the room, came back a couple of minutes later herding Curry in front of him. The rancher looked as if he had been roughly wakened from his sleep. He stared at the men clustered around the burly figure of the lawman, not quite comprehending. Then his gaze narrowed as it fastened on Houston's face.

'All right, what is this, Houston?' he gritted. 'You finally found a way of silencing me before I get a fair trial.'

'Believe me, Curry, I've got nothin' to do with this. You can see for yourself that these men have decided to take the law into their own hands, that they have guns on me. If you reckon I'm fool enough to want to die for a rustler like you, then you're wrong.'

'You're a goddamned liar, Houston,' spat the other. 'You're behind all this. I figure you even got Weston here to change the brands on some of his cattle and then pass the blame to me.'

'Come on,' said Weston harshly, waving the Colt menacingly. 'Get out of here and into the street.'

Curry stood quite still for a long moment, like a man carved from stone, sweat beading his forehead and upper lip. In the silence of the room, there was only the broken breathing of the men. Then, prodded by the gunsight of one of the men, Curry stumbled towards the outer door, moved on to the boardwalk, stood for a while looking about him into the greying light of the dawn. He lifted his gaze momentarily, but only as far as the end of the street where it ran out of the town and into the rocky country to the north, where the big cottonwood stood alone, a solitary sentinel against the undulating skyline. For a second, a shiver went through him, then he swung on Weston and Houston.

'You'll regret this day's work, both of you,' he gritted thinly. 'You're figurin' on stringin' me up from that tree yonder, without a properly appointed trial and on the word of a paid liar.' His tone was both slightly hoarse and hollow sounding.

'You'll get your trial,' Weston said grimly. He turned on Houston. 'As for you, Marshal. This is no further concern of yours. Me and the boys aim to carry out the proceedings from now on without any interference. We're doin' Cross Buttes a favour, gettin' rid of a polecat like this.'

'You're goin' against the law, Weston,' said Houston quietly. 'You realize that and there'll have to be some inquiry into this.'

'Just button your lip, Marshal, and nothin' is goin' to happen to you,' muttered one of the others.

Curry was hustled along the street in the direction of the saloon. Already, the town was coming awake. The citizens learned in some strange manner that Ed Curry had been taken from the jail, that he was to be tried by a court of men under Weston. Whether there was any premonition of shame or fear in the town that morning, it was impossible to tell. Knowing that Weston was to try Curry, few people questioned whether or not it would be a fair trial. But those who expected Houston to take a hand in the proceedings and stop the farce were to be disappointed. He remained shut away in his office throughout the whole of that long, sultry morning.

A little before noon, the batwing doors of the saloon were thrown open and Weston stepped out on to the boardwalk. The crowd which had gathered in the dusty street outside the building gave up a faint sigh as they stared at Weston's face, glazed a little with sweat but with a triumphant smile on his thin lips.

'You know why we took Curry out of jail,' he said loudly so that his words were heard by everyone in the crowd. 'Houston was goin' to hold him until the circuit judge arrived in town. Then he'd stage a big trial. By that time, Curry would have been free, gettin' his men ready, makin' to ride 'em into town and burn the place. He threatened to do that as soon as Houston brought him in. We asked Houston to keep him in jail until the judge came, but since he's got no real proof, he couldn't hold him. So we had to take the law into our own hands, try him ourselves. *And we've found him guilty of rustlin'.*'

He lifted his voice a little towards the end. From beneath lowered lids, he watched the faces of the people in the crowd. If there was to be any trouble, he reckoned, it would come now. There was some talking, a lot of head nodding and shaking, but nobody spoke out openly.

Holding up his hands for silence, he went on: 'We've got a quick way with rustlers here in Cross Buttes. When a man's been found guilty, we hang him. No sense in askin' for trouble and waitin' for his gunhawks to ride into town and burn the place.' He dug into his pocket and came out with the large watch, stared down at it intently for several moments without speaking.

'You goin' to lynch him?' called one of the men in the forefront of the crowd.

Weston grinned mirthlessly and shook his head emphatically. 'This is no lynch mob, Cordell. He's had a trial. Now we're goin' to carry out the sentence.'

'What has Houston got to say about this?' The other wanted to know.

'He wants no part of the deal,' Weston said tersely. 'He doesn't know how to square it with the judge when he gets here. We ain't quite so squeamish. When a thing has to be done, then we just get down to it and do it.'

This time there was a faint murmur of approval from somewhere at the back of the crowd. Weston nodded his head slowly. There was a handful of his own men back there ready to whip up the crowd if there was any sign of flagging, or if it seemed to be hostile to what was happening. Inwardly, Weston felt quite pleased about the way in which everything had worked out. The crowd would not have to be swayed much. Curry had proved to be too big a man for their liking in many ways, and his men had made more than a nuisance of themselves in town on several occasions in the past, shooting up the stores, stopping just short of murder at times. Perhaps some of the more far-seeing people were recognizing the fact that with Curry out of the way for rustling, his men would be disbanded and there would be no more trouble from them.

Further along the street, Houston watched the proceedings from the window of the sheriff's office. He smiled thinly as he noticed how Weston was addressing the crowd. He was genuinely enjoying himself, and his smile had something of pleased amusement in it. Everything was going just as he had planned. With Curry out of the way, there would be nobody in the territory big enough to oppose him and he had arranged things so that none of this could work its way back to him. He had done all he could to prevent those men from taking Curry out of jail and carrying through their plan to lynch the other. He did not anticipate any trouble from Curry's men. By the time they came, it would be all over.

Glancing down at his watch he saw that it lacked five minutes to high noon. The sun was at its zenith now and the shadows were short in the dusty street. The heat haze shimmered all around them, blurring the furthermost details, making the hills on the skyline shake as though seen through a layer of water.

He started a little as he heard the faint roll of knuckles on the street door. He had heard no one coming along the boardwalk outside and had guessed that nearly everyone would be down at the saloon. Opening the door, he saw Dan standing there. The other smiled faintly as he stepped inside.

'I see that Weston is doin' all he's been told,' he said. 'I figure he means to hang Curry at high noon. Fittin' end to him.'

'I wish it was all finished,' grunted the other. He turned and moved back to the window, pressing himself against the wall at the side so that he could peer along the street.

'You worried about those gunslingers of Curry's?'

'In a way,' admitted the other. 'I'd feel a lot happier in my mind if I knew where they were at this moment.'

'Then I'll put your mind at rest. They're out scouring the hills for him. Seems they've somehow figured out that he might have gone ridin' to check the boundary fences and his horse may have thrown him.'

'Now why should they think that?' grunted Chuck harshly. He turned to face the other.

Dan shrugged. 'Could be that somebody mentioned to 'em that Curry was seen headin' up into the hills shortly before nightfall yesterday.'

Chuck pondered that for a long moment, then drew back his lips in a grin.

'You old devil you,' he said, clapping his brother across the shoulders. 'So while they trail the hills lookin' for him, we string him up out yonder. Things couldn't have worked out better for us. I tell you, Dan, we'll soon have all of this territory sewn up so tight that nobody will be able to prise it away from us. It was a lucky day when we stopped off here in Cross Buttes.'

The other nodded slowly, stepped away from the window and lowered himself into the high-backed chair behind the desk, stretching out his legs in front of him. He seemed to lack any interest in what was going on a little further down the street.

The crowd outside the saloon waited, with a growing tenseness hanging in the unmoving air. Most of them knew that they were there to witness a killing and if any of them had little heart for the job, they did not show it outwardly. For a long while, the street seemed to be without any sound at all. Then Weston stepped back to the batwing doors and yelled an order. Two men came barging through holding the rancher tightly by the arms as he struggled fiercely in their grip. Weston grimaced, stepped back a pace as Curry was dragged down into the street and then hauled the thirty yards to the cottonwood. Somebody moved ahead with a rope and tossed it expertly over the out-thrusting branch which overhung the trail at that point. Curry lifted his head, staring at it with wide eyes, his tongue running around his dry lips. He seemed incapable of saying anything, seemed almost oblivious of anything but that tree branch with the riata swinging gently from it, the noose on the end twisted through a running knot.

'Get his horse,' Weston called loudly. He motioned to the bay standing hipshot in front of the saloon.

The horse was brought forward and Curry forced to climb up into the saddle, where his hands were tied behind his back. The rope was slipped around his neck, the big knot just visible close under his right ear.

'All right, Curry,' snarled Weston. 'This is the end of the trail for you. The sort of justice we reserve for rustlin' thieves.'

With an effort, the rancher found his voice. It seemed to rasp from his lungs and along a dry throat. 'All of you folk of Cross Buttes,' he said tightly. 'You're all accessories to murder. This is a frame-up brought about by Weston here. And he's bein' paid to do this by Chuck Houston. I was just a mite too outspoken against him in the past when I tried to warn you that he and his cheatin' brother were out to get the whole of this territory in their hands. You let them get away with this and it will be the end for Cross Buttes, for everyone here.'

'You've said too much already,' snapped Weston. He motioned to the man standing beside the tree. 'Haul on that rope, Job. Let's get this over with.'

Job pulled hard on the rope, made it fast so that the heavy knot moved up against Curry's ear, jerking his head to one side. The crowd watched the proceedings expectantly. Behind them, the whole town lay quiet and hushed in the hot stillness of high noon.

Then Weston stepped forward, the lines of his features

etched tightly across his cheeks. He drew in a deep breath before slapping the horse sharply across the rump. The startled animal leapt forward with a shrill neigh. For a moment of utter stillness the crowd stared as one man at the plunging figure on the end of the rope, at the quivering branch which lay over the trail. Then the movements stopped. Weston passed in front of the hanging man, stared out at the crowd.

'If any more of the men around the town figure that they can rustle cattle from their neighbours, I hope they remember this. Punishment and justice are swift here in Cross Buttes.'

Turning on his heel, he pushed through the crowd. Men moved quickly back from him, almost as if they were now strangely afraid to touch him, even to come into involuntary contact with him. A gap opened up for him and he walked through it, made his way slowly and purposefully along the middle of the street without a single backward glance in the direction of the man they had just killed.

Not until he reached the sheriff's office did he pause, then step up on to the boardwalk. In the shadow cast by the overhanging roof at this point, he was almost completely hidden from the crowd at the far end of the street and could peer out in their direction. Now that it was done, he felt a strange quiver in his body; not quite a feeling of guilt, but of a sudden relaxing of the tension which had been building up inside him ever since they had taken Curry out from the jail. Always, at the back of his mind, there had been the feeling that something would go wrong and now that it was all over, he could scarcely believe that it had been done without a hitch. Pushing open the door of the office with the flat of his hand, he went inside. He gave both of the Houston brothers a quick nod.

'It's done,' he said simply. 'That's the end of Ed Curry.'

TWO

AVENGING GUNS

Frank Slade had excellent eyesight and lying on his stomach atop the flat rock on the lower slopes of the Elklands, he watched the dust cloud in the distance as it grew larger and nearer, trying to make out the individual shapes of the riders. For more than two weeks he had been riding west over the wide deserts until he had seen the shadows of the great hills lift on the horizon behind the vague heat haze. Sundown, he had figured earlier that morning, would see him only a day's ride from Curry's ranch. The last letter he had received from the other had reached him in Dodge more than two months before and now that he had been given orders from the Governor of the territory to ride into a town named Cross Buttes, which Ed had also mentioned in his letter, he had decided to pay a visit to the other on the way.

Eyelids faintly wrinkled at the edges as he peered into the glaring light of the sun, reflected from the rocks close around him, he made out the tight bunch of men, like black dots on the vast stretch of the valley below him. There was a singleness of purpose and design about those men which had first attracted his attention to them. A few moments earlier, he had been drinking from the narrow stream which he had located, running at right angles across the trail through the timber. Under the coppery sky, the riders were now clearly visible but too distant for him to recognize any of them. If they kept going in the direction in which they were headed, they would hit the trail lower down and ride up into the slopes, passing within a few yards of where he lay. He mused on that for a moment, not particularly worried about them, but curious.

Once, during the past two weeks, he had met a single rider, heading east across the vast spread of the plains. They had spent a night together at camp, then parted at sunup and both knew that they would never see the other again. Any other riders he had encountered, had been nothing more substantial than vague smoke blurs in the far distance, patterns of dust that lay athwart the trail, but always too far away to be recognized. He sat back on his haunches and built himself a smoke. He was a tall, lissom man, with a rider's looseness about his build, his face tanned to a deep brown by long years of exposure to the hot sun, eyelids and hair bleached a little by it, eyes themselves a deep piercing blue like those of a bird of prey. The guns at his waist were worn low, tied down, the butts smooth and shiny through long use, the leather of the holsters, polished to a similar smoothness.

The riders below made a wide sweep and curved in on the hill trail until they were directly beneath him, cutting up through the broken brush and boulders which lay strewn over the track. Slowly, Frank got to his feet, drew deep on the cigarette, feeling the high sun burn on his shoulders. Gently, he eased himself off the rock and into the trees, watching the trail. The dull tattoo of hoofs on the dust grew louder.

Dropping the butt of the cigarette into the dirt he ground it out with his heel. His mount was loosely tethered to a branch on one of the trees near the trail. It was impossible for these men to ride by without seeing it; and

32

once they spotted it, they would undoubtedly stop to check on any stranger.

He listened to the horses come on, interest and caution rising together in his mind. Seconds dragged past on leaden feet. Sound and riders came quickly around the bend in the trail less than a hundred yards away. He heard a faint shout from the man in the lead, followed by the thin squeal of leather as the other reined up. Then the man walked his horse forward. He was on guard, not so much suspicious of him but alert to his presence there and a little unsure of him. He said so at once:

'You're a way off the main trail here, mister.'

Slade moved forward, out of the shadow of the timber, his hands well away from the guns in their holsters.

'Any reason why I shouldn't take this trail?'

The other shrugged. Dark eyes roamed over his face and it was evident from his expression that the other was trying to place him, wondering about him, about why he might be there. 'I guess not. We don't have many strangers in these parts and naturally everybody is looked on with a little suspicion.' The other stepped down from his mount. came forward leading it by the bridle. 'You're on the run, I suppose?'

'No, just riding through.'

'Going anywhere in particular?' This time a little of the sharpness was beginning to show through the other's voice.

'Maybe that's my business,' he said thinly.

'Is it?' said the other. 'Now maybe.' He searched Slade with a keen glance that missed nothing and believed less. 'Could be that you're not strange. You don't look like a trail tramp to me.' His gaze lowered. 'But you look like a man who knows how to handle those guns and probably has several times in the past.'

'Meaning?'

'That you may have had somethin' to do with the trouble

over in Cross Buttes; and if you have—' The other did not finish his sentence, but Slade saw his face harden a little.

'I don't see what it has to do with you, but I'm on my way to the Lazy Y ranch. Ed Curry who owns the spread happens to be a friend of mine. I've got a letter here from him asking me to visit him when I'm in the territory.'

He saw the gust of expression that passed swiftly over the man's face, the quick, guarded look he gave the rest of the men in the bunch, still sitting their mounts on the trail, hands across their saddlehorns. Then he looked back.

'I'm Clint McCorg, Ed Curry's foreman,' he said harshly. 'You mind showin' me that letter?'

Slade hesitated, then shrugged, dug into the pocket of his jacket and took out the folded sheet of paper, handed it up to the other. McCorg glanced through it briefly, then handed it back, swung towards the rest of the men. 'Better get down, boys,' he called. 'I reckon this could be the man we're lookin' for.'

Slade tightened his lips under the implications of the other's remark, then relaxed as the other said: 'Ed used to talk about you, Slade. Said that if ever he was in trouble we was to try to get in touch with you, let you know what had happened.'

'And Ed's in trouble now?' Slade said softly.

McCorg bit his lower lip, then said harshly: 'He's dead, Slade.'

'Dead!' Slade felt a sudden coldness on his face, a tightness in his chest. 'How did it happen? Who killed him?'

'There was a bunch of 'em in Cross Buttes,' said the other tightly. 'They had him in jail on a trumped-up charge of rustlin' some of Cal Weston's beef.'

'Ed Curry never rustled anybody's beef in his life,' said Slade tautly. 'I can vouch for that.'

'So can we,' grated the other. 'There's a couple of

range-grabbin' brothers in Cross Buttes, a pair named Houston. One of 'em is a gambler in the saloons. The other has got himself the post of Town Marshal. Between them, they run the town and most of the surroundin' territory. Ed Curry tried to stand up to 'em, tried to warn the townsfolk what was happenin' but they seemed too blind to see what was a-goin' on right under their noses. It must've been Houston who rode out with a bunch of deputies and took Ed back into town with 'em. Then this other bunch busts into the jailhouse and takes out Ed without Houston makin' any play to stop 'em.'

'Go on,' said Slade. His voice was low, filled with menace.

'They held a trial in one of the saloons, found him guilty of rustlin' and took him out at high noon and strung him up from the big cottonwood at the end of the street.'

Slade stood absolutely still for many moments, letting the news sink down into his suddenly numbed mind. It scarcely seemed possible that this could have happened to Ed Curry. He knew that things were getting out of hand in Cross Buttes, which was why the Governor had given him the job of riding in there and cleaning things up. He had been given a free hand in his task, had spurned the offer of a star, knowing that in a case such as this it was far better to ride in unannounced and unknown, to poke around a little before anybody knew what was going on. That way, a man had a chance to learn things he might otherwise never find out if he posed behind a badge.

But if what this man had said was true, if some of the townfolk had strung up Ed Curry without a proper, legal trial, then it had suddenly become a personal thing as far as he was concerned.

'Ed had a daughter, didn't he?' he said at length, turning back from his silent contemplation of the distant hills. 'Does she know what has happened to her father?'

'The last I heard, she'd gone back east,' said McCorg. 'But there was talk a while back that she would be comin' out here in a little while.'

Slade mused on that. 'It's goin' to be hard on Kathy when she gets back to learn this news.' He paused, eyed the men to turn. 'And what about you boys now?'

A faint frown mantled McCorg's grim features. He returned Slade's close scrutiny with something close to puzzlement. 'What can we do, mister? Curry's dead and there's no job now for us at the Lazy Y.'

'There could be,' Slade countered. 'Whoever had Curry killed wanted him out of the way pretty badly. It could be because they want to take over the Lazy Y ranch before Miss Kathy gets back to handle her Pa's affairs. I'd call it a favour if you'd ride back with me and stay on until things are straightened out.'

McCorg rubbed his chin for a moment. 'Well . . . I don't rightly know,' he said, his voice fading a little. It was clear that this was something he had not considered. 'Maybe we could do that. You intend to get word to Miss Kathy?'

Slade nodded. 'I'll send her a telegram from the telegraph station.'

There was a murmur of assent from the men and McCorg nodded his head finally.

'Very well, Slade. We'll ride back with you and stay on until Miss Kathy gets back.' He gave a lop-sided grin. 'Besides, we want to know who killed Ed Curry, not the man who pulled the rope, but the real murderer behind that lynching. Then we may have another chore on our hands.'

Slade considered that for a moment, then shook his head. 'No,' he said flatly. 'I know how you all feel about this killing, but the man behind it all is mine. Ed Curry was my closest friend. I've known him for many years now and he saved my life on at least two occasions. I figure it's up to me to bring his killer to justice.'

McCorg shrugged. 'You won't find it easy to get any of the townfolk in Cross Buttes to talk. They're all scared. It's easy to see that from the way they stood by and let Weston do this.'

'Just who is this *hombre*, Weston?' Slade asked as he whistled up his mount, bent to tighten the cinch, then swung up easily into the saddle.

'He's the rancher who owns the spread bordering on Curry's,' said McCorg. He motioned to the rest of the men and they rode out of the small clearing beside the trail, splashed through the shallow stream that ran swiftly down from the high peaks of the Elklands, and up into the timber on the other side, taking the downgrade once more, heading towards the wide valley below.

'Then you could be right.' Slade nodded. 'He isn't the brains behind this. I reckon I'd better have a talk with those two brothers when I get into town.'

'Tread warily in Cross Buttes.' said the foreman warningly. 'It's one hell of a town. Every stranger who rides in is watched continually. Move easily until you know where you stand. Every time I ride down that main street I wonder when somethin' is goin' to bust wide open.'

'It's awfully easy to get in with the wrong crowd there,' said one of the other men.

Ten minutes later they rode out of the timber, through the scattered boulders of the rising foothills and out into the plains.

Slade finished the meal which had been cooked for the returning men that evening, then stepped out on to the veranda of the ranch house. There was a cool wind blowing through the valley now that the sun had gone down and the smell of sage hung in the air, blended with other scents which he only half recognized. In the deep purple dusk, a deep silence hung over the land, broken only by the movement of the horses in the corral and the faint lowing of the herd on the lee of the hill overlooking the valley. Slade's brows drew together as he rolled a cigarette, struck the match on the side of the doorpost and drew smoke deeply into his lungs. This was a beautiful, prosperous valley and he could understand avaricious men casting greedy, envious eyes on it. But was that the real reason behind Ed Curry's untimely death? Somehow, he did not think so. There was more to this killing than that.

There was a sudden movement at the corner of the house and a moment later, Slim Carew, the cook, came into sight. He paused for a moment as he saw Slade standing there, then came on, wiping his hands on the wide, long apron he wore around his middle.

'I was hopin' I'd find you here, Mister Slade,' he said quietly. 'I recollect Mister Curry talkin' about you at times. He had a high opinion of you.'

'I'm glad to hear that.' Slade's gaze turned a little smoky. 'You know anythin' of how he died?'

Carew peered into the dimness that lay over the valley, his face tight, the deep lines etched into the flesh around his mouth and the corners of his eyes.

'A bunch of men ridin' with the Town Marshal rode up, asked him to go with 'em into town. There was some talk about rustlin' steers off Weston's land, but I was through in the kitchen at the back of the house when it happened and I didn't hear what they were sayin' too good. They had guns on him, so he had to go with 'em. The rest, I know only from what I've heard in town. The marshal had him locked away in the jail, but that night a group of men led by Weston took him out at gunpoint, held a mock trial in the saloon, found him guilty of the charge and strung him up at high noon.'

'And the Town Marshal made no attempt to stop it?'

'That's right, I guess.' Carew wagged his head. 'You thinkin' of ridin' into town and makin' trouble?' His glance was shrewd beneath the thick, heavy brows.

'If I did, it might make him rest a little easier, Slim.'

'Could be. But the dead are dead, Mister Slade, and nothin' you can do will bring him back. And then there's Miss Kathy to consider.'

'Where does she fit into it?'

'Could be that she won't want any more trouble with the townsfolk if she means to stay on here and run the ranch like her Pa did.'

Slade smiled grimly, blew smoke into the air. 'I only remember her as a girl with her hair in braids,' he confessed. 'But even then she struck me as the kind of girl who wouldn't buckle down to anythin' like this. She's like her father. I reckon she'll want the killers found and punished.'

'Sure, but she'll want it done the legal way.' His gaze settled on Slade's face once more. 'Everybody knows the sort of men those Houston brothers are. Could be that the townsfolk have realized they made a mistake electin' Chuck Houston as marshal. If so, they might decide to put a better man into office. You might qualify for the job and then you could do this legally.'

Slade shook his head. 'I want no part of the law in this town. Ed was no rustler and somebody in that lynch mob must know who paid them to kill him.'

'The rumours are that it was Chuck Houston.'

'That isn't evidence. I'd need proof before I could do anythin'.'

'As far as I know, not a single soul in town would tell you what you want to know. They are all too afraid of Houston. You can ferret around and try to find out somethin' but I don't give much for your chances.'

'It could be I may be able to force their hand.' Slade crushed out the butt of his cigarette, moved down into the courtyard. 'I shall ride into Cross Buttes at sunup.'

'You want me to get the boys to ride with you?'

Slade shook his head once more. 'What I have to do is

best done alone,' he said. He kept his smile as he talked. It was a hard smile; it had threat and weight. Carew continued to watch him as he walked slowly over the courtyard to pause by the fence of the corral. Very slowly, it came to him the kind of man that Frank Slade was, something that Ed Curry had never talked about. In spite of the fact that he was merely the cook here, had been for the past fifteen years, he was a good judge of men and he knew what the thing was that set Frank Slade apart from most other men he knew. The other was completely co-ordinated, was a fighting machine, confident and utterly deadly.

Inside or outside the law, he thought with a faint shiver in his mind, men like this were always killers. It came to him that the darkness was unnaturally still over the ranch and he paused for only a moment before stepping inside.

At first light, Slade saddled and rode out of the dusty courtyard, taking the narrow, twisting trail which eventually led to Cross Buttes. At the edge of the spread, he put his mount across a gravel-bottomed ford and then deliberately left the trail, not intending to rejoin it until he came within sight of the town. Deep in the tall first-growth pines which bordered the higher ground, he rode while the sunlight filtered through the lower branches, the sun itself lifting higher into the cloudless heavens. Beneath his horse's feet, the thick mat of pine needles muffled its hoofbeats, making scarcely a sound, and there was only the scuffle of birds in the higher branches to break the clinging green stillness.

The aromatic smell of the pines filled his nostrils for most of the morning. Occasionally, he paused whenever he passed over another trail, but there was no indication of any other riders in this part of the hills and although he rode without haste, there was a restlessness bubbling up inside him which could not be denied. The news of Ed Curry's death, particularly the manner in which it had

40

occurred, had touched him more deeply than he had realized. The immediate desire to destroy the men responsible, which he had experienced on hearing the news, had faded a little now, seemed less than enough for such men. All the long hours of thinking about it, remembering Ed Curry as he had been in the old days, and thinking of his daughter Kathy, made it necessary that these men should face their crime, should suffer from it, knowing that they could not escape the vengeance which was soon to befall them.

He thought back once more to the meeting he had had with the Governor. There had been concern expressed over the lawless elements along this part of the frontier, the necessity of stamping it out, of making these small, sometimes isolated, frontier towns safe for decent people to live in, so that civilisation might continue westward and the country as a whole progress towards the fulfilment of that earlier dream which had sent the pioneers heading west in a great flood, which had been truly described as the greatest exodus of all time.

At first, Governor Wallis had wanted to pin a badge on him, confirm the position as law officer, but Slade had declined this, believing that it would be possible for him to work better under cover, with nobody knowing who he was, or what his purpose there might be. At first, it had seemed like just another job to be done, with the chance of meeting his old friend, Ed Curry, once more; but now this mission was something much more personal and because of that he knew he had to be more careful than ever, otherwise emotion would tend to blur his actions and lead him into trouble.

He threw off several more creeks before high noon. When he finally came out of the timber, after making camp by a clear, fast-running stream, the sun had passed its zenith, was weltering slowly, dipping down the long slide of the sky, but the heat still remained, shimmering on

41

the skyline, the sunlight harsh and dazzling, blinding on the eye. The metal bits of his bridle sent stabs of hurting brilliance into his eyes and grew hot to the touch. Nothing relieved the heat head as it lifted to its piled-up intensity, the burning pressure lying on his head and shoulders, pressing on him like the flat of a mighty hand.

Inwardly, he felt glad when he sighted the dark blur of shadow on the horizon, knew that he was within sight of Cross Buttes. He felt the tightness grow in his chest, pulling the muscles tight under his throat. The hills went before him, lifting in grey and purple shadow with the yellow scar of the trail running ahead of him, vanishing into the shimmering mists. The sun now shone directly into his eyes as it dropped towards the crests of the hills beyond the town and he hooded his lids against the harsh light.

Crossing a low rise, he rode into the main street of Cross Buttes, letting his glance wander seemingly idly from side to side, his keen glance missing nothing, noticing the horses tethered in front of the saloons, a few standing hipshot too in front of the hotel. Several idlers sat in the shade of the boardwalk, their high-backed chairs tilted back, some with their hats placed over their faces, others following the tall man who rode his roan quietly through the town.

Drawing up in front of the livery stables, he swung down, hitched the gunbelt a little higher about his middle, then led his mount inside. The stables were cooler than the street outside and there was the smell of hay and horses there.

A droop-moustached hostler came from the back, gave him a quick, birdlike glance, then took the reins from him. The other's glance, roving over the horse, noticed the trail dust on the animal's flanks and he nodded knowingly.

'Ridden some distance today, mister,' he said, hopefully, head cocked a little on one side.

'That's right,' said Slade shortly. He tossed the other a coin. 'Better cool him off a little before you give him a feed.'

'Sure thing. You intend stayin' long in town?'

'I might,' Slade nodded. 'Depends on how soon I finish my business.'

The other's glance was suddenly both covert and uncomfortable. He said in a low, hushed tone: 'You ain't a lawman, are you, mister?'

'Now why should I be a lawman?' Slade set his lips tight, gave the other a closely appraising look. Very often in a town like this the blacksmith and the hostler were the two men who seemed to pick up all of the information and news. 'I kind of figured there was a Town Marshal here, Leastways, so I heard.'

'We've got Chuck Houston.' The other spat into the dirt at his feet. 'But he ain't no real lawman. We had a lynchin' here some time back, but did he make any attempt to stop it? No, sir.'

'Maybe there was too many of 'em,' suggested Slade conversationally.

'Weren't that at all. Those men in the lynchin' party were friends of Houston's. He could've stopped that hangin' if he'd had a mind to.'

'You got any proof of that?' Slade said tersely.

The other made to say something, then threw a quick glance over Slade's shoulder, shut his lips tightly and moved back, further into the shadows of the stables. Slade turned very slowly. At first, he could see nothing in the street to account for the other's curious behaviour. Then he saw the bulky figure that had stepped through the door of the sheriff's office across the street and was angling towards them. The hostler moved back into the stables, towards the stalls. Evidently this could mean trouble and he wanted none of it.

The other man stopped in the street a couple of yards

43

away, hands close to his gunbelt, fingers curled a little. When he spoke, his voice was without inflection.

'You just ridden into town, mister?' he asked, not for one second taking his eyes off Slade.

'That's right. You got any objection?'

The cool, impersonal insolence in the other's voice stung the other. His lips drew tight and a red flush rose from his neck, suffusing his broad, fleshy features. 'What's your name, mister and what business have you got in town?'

Slade lifted his brows a little, then grinned slightly. 'The name's Frank Slade. My business in Cross Buttes is personal.'

The other was not satisfied with this. He went on in the same, cold voice: 'Now maybe it is, and maybe it isn't, Mister Slade. But I happen to be the marshal here and it's up to me to see that law and order is kept in the town. If you came here lookin' for trouble, then my advice to you is get back to your horse and dust on out of here pronto.'

'And if I choose to stay?'

'Then, by God, I'll lock you in jail until you do see sense.'

'Like you did Ed Curry.' Slade let the words drop like pieces of iron into the silence. He saw the other start at the mention of Curry's name, saw the look of sudden awareness that came to his face.

'What do you know about Ed Curry?' he snapped harshly.

Slade shrugged. 'Only what I've heard. They say that he was lynched by some hotheads who dragged him out of jail and tried him by their own law. Seems that the law itself did nothing to stop 'em. Is that what happens to everybody you lock up inside your jail, Marshal?'

There was an abrupt change in the atmosphere. The marshal seemed to have realized that the man who faced him was not the ordinary run of cowboys who drifted into

44

town to spend their pay and then leave when the money was gone. This man was quite a different proposition and for the moment he was a little unsure how to deal with him.

'Mister, I'm tellin' you for the last time. Watch yourself so long as you're in town. If you step out of line just once, I'll be lookin' for you.'

For a moment longer, the other stood facing him, his face dull with anger and bafflement. Then he spun sharply on his heel and walked back to the office across the street, not once looking back.

Slade hesitated for a moment, then ambled in the direction of the small restaurant which he had noticed when he had ridden in. Pushing open the door with the flat of his hand, he went inside, ordered bacon, eggs and fried potatoes, with coffee, and sat down near the window. The place was almost deserted. A couple of grizzled prospectors were seated at the table nearest the door, but apart from them the place was empty.

The food came five minutes later and he ate with relish, then sat back, allowing his muscles to loosen, enjoying the feeling of relaxation after the long ride from the Lazy Y. The food made his feel more restless, brought his brows together into a long line, furrowing his brow.

He built himself a smoke, then pushed back his chair, got to his feet and walked over to the counter. He moved with the easy grace of a fully confident man, quiet and deadly, and it was this characteristic of him which the man behind the counter noticed at once. Slade turned his smoky gaze on the other. 'I'd like a little information,' he said, his voice vibrant and strangely compelling.

The barkeep's face turned a shade paler than before. 'What do you want to know, mister?'

'I'm lookin' for a man named Cal Weston. I figure he's probably in town somewhere.'

The other hesitated a few moments longer than was

necessary. 'Weston?' he murmured numbly, staring down at the backs of his hands where they rested on the polished counter in front of him. 'I'd say he was at his ranch. It's along the south-east trail about five miles out of town. You can't miss it if you keep riding in that direction and—'

'I said I've got reason to believe that he's still in town,' Slade said firmly. Some of the steel was beginning to show through the seeming indifference of his tone and the other seemed to recognize it, for he said, licking his lips nervously, 'If he is in town, mister, then I reckon the place you'll probably find him will be in the saloon at the east end of town.'

'Thanks.' Slade nodded. He stepped back from the counter, then asked in a calm tone: 'What's botherin' you, old-timer? You seem to have somethin' on your mind.'

'It's nothin',' quavered the other, his face blanched. 'Just that nobody comes ridin' in town askin' for Weston unless it means trouble.'

'Very likely that's because he's in with the Houston brothers,' Slade suggested, watching the other's reactions closely.

The man's lips drew together in a tight line. For a moment, his gaze held Slade's then he looked away, confused. 'I wouldn't know too much about that,' he murmured, running the tip of his tongue around his dry lips. 'There are a lot of things happen here in town that nobody wants to know about.'

'The lynchin' of Ed Curry for one?' Slade stared up into the other's face.

'That had nothin' to do with the likes of me, mister.' The barkeep made a gesture with his hands. 'We're just the little men here. We got no say in what goes on.'

'Then if it's against the law, it's about time you made it your business,' Slade grated. He jammed his hat down a little further on his head, moved to the door. Turning, he said in a soft voice, very soft: 'You think I might find Dan Houston in the saloon?'

'Possibly.' The barkeep's tone was non-committal. 'But he's a bad man to go up against, a real killer.'

Slade squinted at the other for a second, grinned lopsided. 'I had that figured already, mister,' he said. The doors swung shut behind him as he stepped out on to the boardwalk.

Cross Buttes dozed in the purple shadows which now lay athwart the trail. There was a coolness flowing down from the distant hills. Slade could feel it on his face as he left his mount tethered outside the restaurant and made his way along the street to the saloon. Already, there was the sound of music and merriment coming from the place, the tinkling notes of a tinny piano sounding above the harsh yelling and singing. Elsewhere in Cross Buttes there were a few shadows, standing motionless in the deep shadows outside the various buildings, men taking it easy now that the blistering heat of the day had dissipated. There was, he noticed, a light burning inside the sheriff's office further along the street and he guessed that the other half of the Houston duo was still there. Maybe the Town Marshal was thumbing through his wanted posters, looking for his face, Slade thought with a faint sense of grim amusement. If that were the case, he would find nothing.

He pushed open the doors of the saloon with the flat of his hand and went inside. There were several card games going on inside the saloon and Slade let his glance slide over them before finally settling on that which was taking place in the far corner. The man dealing the cards was thin-faced, wore a black frock coat and now that he was seeing the other for the first time, Slade was able to see the vague resemblance between the other and the Town Marshal. Certainly the other was burly, broadshouldered and florid-featured, but Slade did not have to appraise the other twice to know that this was Dan Houston, the man he was seeking.

Letting his gaze drift away, he moved across to the bar, leaned his weight on it and lifted a finger to the bartender. The other came across. He was a big man, had once been lean-hipped and well-muscled. but long years behind the bar had left their mark on him and he had run to fat now. But he was still a man to be reckoned with in a brawl, Slade decided.

'What'll it be, stranger?' asked the other.

'Sour mash,' Slade said. As the other brought up the bottle from under the counter and set it down, together with a glass in front of him, Slade caught hold of the bottle neck.

'Leave it here,' he said quietly, his voice very low.

'All right.' There was a speculative gleam in the bartender's eyes. He paused and looked up more closely at Slade, watching the other's unblinking gaze, and read death there. He inched back a little behind the bar, said in a hoarse whisper: 'Whoever you're lookin' for, mister, I want no trouble here.'

'There won't be,' Slade said shortly. 'Unless somebody else starts it.' He moved his gaze a fraction, over the barkeep's shoulder, watching Houston's image in the mirror along the back. It was a huge, ornate piece of glass that must have cost a fortune to bring out to Cross Buttes and set it up in its present position. Delicate metal filigree designs edged it and the glass itself was virtually flawless.

He saw that Houston had paused, holding his cards in front of him, was eyeing him curiously, a black cheroot clamped between his thin lips, his eyes narrowed down to mere slits.

Slade poured himself a drink, tossed the liquor down in a single gulp, felt it burn his mouth and the back of his throat on the way down. He gave no sign that he was aware of Dan Houston's close scrutiny. The other watched him for several seconds, then went on with the game as one of the other men at the table said something to him in a low tone.

The bartender gave him a sudden head-on glance,

following the direction of Slade's gaze through the mirror.

'You're lookin' for big trouble if you tangle with him, mister,' he said in a hoarse whisper. 'That's Dan Houston, brother of the Town Marshal. One word from him and you'll find yourself tossed into the jailhouse and there you'll stay until the circuit judge gets here. Could be they'll forget you're there and you'll rot in one of the cells until they decide to bring you to trial.'

'I think,' said Slade slowly, 'that Houston will find it more difficult to put me in jail than he did with Ed Curry.'

'You were a friend of Ed Curry's?'

Slade's hard stare turned slightly ironic. 'Seems to me that when he had need of friends, there was nobody around. But like you said, he was a friend of mine. And I don't like what happened to him here in town.'

'Don't try to force your hand with him, mister.' There was no mistaking the concern in the other's tone now. 'He's got friends with him. Even if you kill him, and he's deadly fast with a gun, it won't be the end of anythin'. Chuck Houston will stop at nothin' then to gun you down. '

'I guess that's a risk I'll have to take,' said the tall man easily. He poured a second drink, drank it down, tossed a couple of coins on to the bar and then swung away, walking among the round tables towards that at which Dan Houston sat. He knew instinctively that the other was aware of him, even though the gambler did not look up as he approached. Not until Slade stopped immediately opposite the other, did Houston glance up, his gaze slightly puzzled. There was no recognition, no fear in his eyes as he let his gaze wander over the tall, rangy man who stood in front of him.

Taking the cheroot from between his lips, he said thinly: 'You lookin' for somebody, friend?'

'That's right,' Slade nodded. 'I'm lookin' for the murderin' sidewinders who killed Ed Curry.'

The saloon became tomb-like. Nobody moved and not

a single word was spoken for a long time. Then Houston shifted his body in his chair, laid his cards face-downwards on the table in front of him. 'You a friend of that rustler?'

Slade drew in his breath sharply, then forced steadiness into himself. He recognized that the other was deliberately trying to anger him, kept all emotion out of his face. 'Seems to me you've got your sense of values mixed up a little, Houston. And from what I've heard I don't recollect there being any trial before he was lynched.'

'If you're so het up about it, why not see the man responsible,' sneered the other. 'I had nothin' to do with it. Weston was the man who made the charge of rustlin' and he carried out the trial and the sentence.'

'So I heard,' Slade went on evenly. 'But like I said, I aim to find the men who arranged Ed Curry's murder. Weston was just the instrument of it and soon his turn will come. But to my way of thinkin', there were only two men behind the killin'. Two men who want this territory for themselves. You and your brother, Houston!'

Dan Houston's face twisted into a mask of anger and Slade saw the dark colour stain his cheeks. 'You've got a lot of nerve comin' in here and makin' these threats and accusations, mister,' he snarled. 'Who the hell are you and what is this to do with you?'

'The name is Slade. Like I said, Curry was my friend and I know that he was no rustler.'

Lithely, Houston got to his feet, pushing back his chair. 'Listen, friend,' he said thinly. 'Don't bite off more'n you can chew. If you're figurin' on makin' any trouble around here then we can soon arrange for a site in Boot Hill for you. Tuck in your tail and ride on out of here before you join your friend, Curry,'

Slade shook his head. He said tightly, speaking through his teeth: 'You're a fool, Houston. You're the kingpins here only so long as nobody dares to go against you. But if you figure that any of these men here are goin' to risk their lives to back your actions, you're dead wrong. This isn't their fight. This is just somethin' between you and me.'

Houston jerked upright and gave that idea some thought. He turned his head very slowly from one side to the other, letting his glance pass over the faces of the men seated at the other tables. What he saw there must have finally convinced him that Slade had spoken the truth. Still there was no fear in his eyes, only a more acute awareness as he studied Slade more closely.

For a long moment there was no sound in the saloon. Even outside, in the street, every sound seemed to have faded into insignificance. Then Houston said thinly: 'Mister, I'm goin' to walk outside that door. If you've got the guts you say you have, I'll be expectin' you outside in the street.'

Slade nodded. 'I'll be there,' he said tightly.

Houston considered Slade's face for a moment, then he edged around the side of the table and walked slowly and deliberately for the door without once looking round. Slade watched him go, watched the doors swung shut behind the other. He was still alert for treachery. He recognized the other's type, had come up against such men several times in the past. Men fast with a gun but not daring to face up squarely to a man who might be as fast, or faster, than they were. There was a fresh current of excitement running through him as he stood there, knowing that every eye in the saloon was on him.

As he moved for the door, hitching the heavy gunbelt a little higher around his waist, the man behind the bar said tersely: 'I don't know who you are, Slade, or why you've decided to ride in here and poke your nose into this business. but I do like to see fair play. Don't trust Houston. He'll have something set up for you out there. Be careful.'

'Thanks for the warnin',' Slade nodded. He stepped up to the doors, paused for a moment and then swung them open, stepping out on to the boardwalk outside.

THREE

THROW A FAST GUN

It was too quiet.

Cross Buttes lay in the dimness of dusk and nothing moved on the street or along the wooden boardwalks. This was the time of evening when the birds went to rest, just before the coyote began to wail out on the prairie beyond the town. Slade stood quite still, looking about him, eyes becoming swiftly accustomed to the darkness. His gaze wandered over the shadow-filled world of the street and the dark houses on either side, knowing that danger lurked there, that the bartender had spoken the truth and Dan Houston did not intend to meet him on even terms. There was no movement in front of him, no man-shaped silhouette, waiting in the middle of the street for him. Houston had walked through the doors of the saloon and vanished utterly. Slade did not doubt that the other was lying in wait for him in the black mouth of one of the narrow alleys which opened off the main street.

Seconds passed, lengthening towards a minute since he had stepped into the open. He could feel the tension begin to grow. A quick glance over his shoulder and he saw the heads of men peering over the curving doors of the saloon, others at the windows which looked directly out on to the street. They too, he thought grimly, now knew Houston for a coward, a bushwhacker who fired from the darkness, not daring to fight on even terms. Slade felt cramped and taut as he stood there, waiting. He breathed deeply for half a dozen breaths, then stepped off into the growing darkness which had settled silently over the town. His eyes were never still. From past experience he knew how fatal it could be to stare at one spot for any length of time in the darkness. Even though he was in the open, Slade felt curiously less conspicuous in the protective dimness. He had no certain knowledge that Dan Houston had not moved off quickly once he had left the saloon, to warn his brother of what had happened. For all he knew, he might have to face both of the Houston brothers out here in the darkness, one of them setting him up while the other, moving around in the maze of alleys, shot him from the shadows.

He reached the point where one of the alleys, branching off from the main street, opened out like a gaping black mouth between two of the buildings. He paused at the intersection, only long enough to ascertain that it was safe for him to go on. Even as he hesitated, it came to him that Houston might have circled around, might be behind him, rather than somewhere in front of him. But he put that thought out of his mind right away. He had enough on his mind without troubling about that possibility. Sprinting across the open stretch of ground, he made it clear of the alley without any shot coming from the darkness. Here he went slower, feeling his way. Then he stopped. There was a sudden movement on the boardwalk. A shadow moved close to a round water butt. Slade whirled, hands moving towards the guns in their holsters, then paused, his heart racing as he saw the drunk stagger away from the wall where he had been steadying himself. The other lurched down into the street, staggered towards him.

Slade cursed under his breath. This was the last thing he wanted; anyone else in the street at this time. Houston would make the most of an opportunity like this, relying on Slade hesitating to shoot with an innocent bystander so close to the field of fire. The drunk reeled closer, swaying from side to side as he approached. Sucking in a deep breath, acutely aware of his precarious position, Slade hissed: 'Get away from me, you fool, unless you want to get yourself killed.'

The man moved right up to him. Slade could smell the overpowering reek of whiskey on the other's breath. He made to thrust the other away, then withdrew his hand as he caught the harsh, hoarse whisper: 'Watch your step, stranger. I just saw Dan Houston go into the alley a few yards along the street. Reckon it could be you he was waitin' for.'

Slade tightened his lips. 'Thanks,' he said shortly. 'Now get off the street. There'll be gunplay here soon.'

Still swaying a little, but not as much as before, the other lurched away, staggered up on to the boardwalk, clung to one of the wooden uprights for a long moment, and then vanished into the gloom which lay like a deep velvet blanket over everything. Standing there, tensed and alert, Slade made a leisurely examination of the stretch of street which lay ahead of him. He made out the dark, gaping mouth of the alley, less than twenty yards ahead of him to his right. If Houston was compelled to make a run for it, he would be able to make it back along the narrow alley and into the rabbit-warren of similar openings further back from the main street.

There was a pile of rough-sawn logs near the entrance to the alley and it struck Slade that this was where a would-be assassin would lie in wait. Cautiously he went forward in a half crouch. Soon it would occur to Houston that Slade knew his hiding place and the other would be forced to make his play. This was the moment that Slade was waiting for. He had carefully edged in to the side of the street so as to present a more difficult target to the waiting killer. The little spot between his shoulder blades began to itch. It was a feeling he had learned never to ignore.

'Step out into the street and face me like a man, Houston,' he called loudly, knowing that his voice would carry to the men behind him near the saloon, might sting Houston into doing something unthinkingly.

Almost at once, before the echoes of his words had died away among the still buildings. a gunshot blew the night asunder. Slade saw the lancing tongue of blue-crimson flame that lanced from the muzzle of the killer's gun. Unhit, he threw himself down, heard the hum of the slug as it tore through the air immediately above his prone body. Twisting as he hit the ground, he jerked the Colt from its holster, threw two swift shots in the direction of the pile of logs, heard one chip wood from the natural barricade, then the other make a tearing, meaty sound as it found its target. There came an oddly muffled grunt from the hidden man, the sound of a heavy body falling against wood. Some of the logs, dislodged from the pile, fell to the ground and rolled across the street.

Cautiously, alert for any trick, Slade eased himself to his feet, went forward, the pistol cocked in his hand, finger bar-straight in the trigger. In the gloom, he could just make out the dark shape of the fallen man, lying across the top of the logs. From behind him came the sound of running feet. Far off in the distance, a man yelled once, loud and clear, the sound carrying easily in the dark stillness of the night. The echoing clamour of the gunshots, coming so swiftly on each other, had faded into silence among the houses.

'Houston,' said Slade quietly. He levelled the barrel of the Colt on the other.

There was no sound from the gunman. Reaching him, Slade bent, still alert for treachery. Two men came rushing up at his heels. One said harshly: 'Better get the doctor here, Slim.'

'No need for that,' Slade said calmly. 'He's dead.'

There was a taut, strained silence from the small crowd which had now gathered around him, a crowd of men who seemed to have sprung up from nowhere. Then one of the men cleared his throat noisily. 'You're sure started somethin' now, mister,' he said ominously. 'Wait until Chuck Houston gets to hear about this.'

Slade straightened, thrust the Colt back into its holster. He knew that perhaps he should have felt some sensation of exhilaration, knowing that one of Ed Curry's murderers had been killed, but there was only a vague, overall emptiness in him. He knew enough of the explosive situation in this hell town, to realize that what the man in the crowd had said was true. This was not the end of anything, it was only the beginning. There would be a lot more blood spilt before it was finished.

Heavy footsteps sounded on the wooden boardwalk and the burly figure of Chuck Houston came pushing his way through the wall of men surrounding the alley mouth.

Silently, the Town Marshal bent beside the dead body of his brother. For a long moment, he crouched there, feeling the pulse, then he got to his feet and stared at the men around him.

'Who did this?' he rasped tautly.

'I did,' Slade said quietly. 'He called me out in the saloon down the street and then tried to bushwhack me here instead of facing me down like a man. He shot at me first.'

'You're a liar, mister,' snapped the other. He seemed beside himself with fury and his right hand hovered dangerously close to the butt of the gun at his waist. 'You shot him down in cold blood. I warned you when you rode into town that if you started any trouble here in Cross Buttes, I'd—'

'Easy now, Marshal,' said one of the men hesitantly. 'It all happened like he said. Dan called him out in the saloon, said he'd step outside and wait for him. Seems he changed his mind and—'

'You stay out of this, Curtis.' Houston whirled on the man who had spoken, sent the other cringing back into the crowd with a single, burning glance. 'I say that this *hombre* shot down Dan in cold blood. We got only one law here for gunslingers and I'm goin' to—'

'Hold it right there, Houston,' Slade said coldly. The icy quality of his voice stopped the other in the act of making a move for his gun. 'Go for that gun or back down. I say that your brother was one of the men behind the killin' of Ed Curry. You know who the others are. And I wouldn't advise you to try to stop me from ridin' out of town. I won't have any hesitation about killin' you too.'

'You'll regret this night's work,' hissed the other. For a moment, his face hardened and the thought of action lived in his eyes. Then he lowered his hunched shoulders a fraction. 'You don't have a chance of gettin' out of this territory and come first light, I'm gettin' a posse sworn in to hunt you down. I'll kill you if it's the last thing I do.'

'Come lookin' for me and it will be,' Slade said ominously. 'I'm takin' over the Lazy Y until Curry's daughter gets here and I've got a bunch of men out there who're just itchin' to ride out here and take this town apart. You'd better start prayin' that I can keep 'em on a tight rein or your life ain't goin' to be worth a plugged nickel.' He saw by the expression on the other's face that his words had made their impression. Without turning, he backed away along the street. He felt reasonably certain that he had nothing to fear from the men who stood around, but there was always the chance that Houston might try a suicidal attempt to avenge his brother there and then.

Reaching the livery stable, he backed inside, then thrust the Colt back into its holster, moved quickly to the stalls, picked out his horse, swung the saddle into place and tightened the cinch quickly. There was no sound from outside in the street. Climbing into the saddle, he rode the horse to the entrance, lowered his head as he passed through, and wheeled the mount sharply along the street, hunched forward in the saddle. One stray shot came after him and before he reached the end of the street he heard the marshal's bull-like voice roaring at the men. Slade did not wait to see whether any of the men would follow the marshal, but gave his horse its head.

There was no moon that night, but the stars were clear and bright, scattered in a powdering of silver across the majestic arch of the heavens. In the shimmering starglow, Slade was able to make out the trail, to follow it with little difficulty. Swinging in a wide circle, he crossed the hills and hit the lower reaches a little before midnight. A coldness swept down on him from the higher slopes and there was a dampness in the air as he rode alongside the bank of a wide, sluggish river. He rode quickly, but cautiously, keeping his eyes and ears open, not ruling out the possibility of Houston managing to get some men to follow him. If he did, they would ride hard, pushing their horses to the limit in a bid to catch up with him before he reached the Lazy Y ranch. Chuck Houston would never rest until he had avenged his brother's death. Maybe, Slade thought, it would have simplified matters if he had called the other out back there and killed two birds with one stone, but that would have been too easy. He wanted Chuck Houston, whom he guessed to have been the real brains behind the murder of Ed Curry, to die slowly, to know that death was approaching, to recognize the inevitability of it, he fact that it was something he could not escape no matter how hard he tried. He wanted Houston to suffer as Ed Curry had suffered during those hours he had spent in jail.

Riding down the slope into an old buffalo-wallow, he

crossed it quickly and kept to the low ground, occasionally throwing a quick look over his shoulder, watchful for any sign of pursuit. But there was none and a little after five o'clock in the morning, he rode into the courtyard of the Lazy Y ranch. Letting his mount loose into the corral, he made his way slowly towards the house. As he approached, a shadow lifted from the porch. Slade caught a glimpse of the glowing tip of a cigarette, saw the rifle held in the crook of the other's elbow and knew that the ranch was not quite as deserted as it had appeared to be when he had ridden in.

McCorg stepped down from the porch, nodded a greeting to Slade. 'Thought it was you as soon as you came over the skyline yonder,' he affirmed. 'You bein' followed?'

'Could be,' Slade acknowledged. He paused for a moment and then said in a low, quiet voice: 'Dan Houston's dead. He called me out in the saloon, tried to shoot me down from cover.'

'And Chuck Houston?' The foreman's voice had grown suddenly hard and tight. 'Does he know what happened?'

Slade nodded. 'He knows. He's sworn to kill me. He may have got a posse together and be on my trail. It's doubtful if he'll ride in here. He knows we'll be ready for him and he won't get enough men to follow him to take us.'

'Chuck Houston is a dangerous man. About as cunnin' as a rattler. I know what I'm talkin' about. Better watch how you tread around here from now on. There are some men who'll throw in their lot with him, Cal Weston and his crew. They're in this now as deep as Houston is. They have no other choice but to do as he says.'

Slade nodded grimly. It was what he had expected. 'I reckon I'll try to get some sleep before dawn,' he said, moving up on to the veranda. 'It's been a long night.'

'Sure,' McCorg nodded. 'I'll keep watch until daylight. Those *hombres* may have decided to trail you, hopin' to take us by surprise.'

Slade went into the house. There was a lamp burning on the table in the parlour throwing a pale yellow radiance through the room and out into the corridor. He made his way to the back of the house, feeling easier in his mind knowing that McCorg was out there, keeping watch. The other was competent and able, not the sort of man to fall asleep when he was on watch.

He did not bother to light the lamp in the bedroom, but took off his clothes and stretched himself out wearily on the low iron bed in the corner. It was still dark outside, but the stars seemed to be paling a little towards the east, heralding an early dawn. Many times on the trail, he had been able to snatch just a couple of hours sleep and it had become a habit with him, this ability to fall asleep at once, almost at will. He did it now, waking three hours later to find the first red rays of the rising sun slanting in through the window, painting a pattern of crimson on the far wall.

The three hours sleep had been sufficient to refresh him and he swung his legs to the floor, went over to the wash basin near the window and washed the trail dust from his face and neck. The soap stung his skin but made him feel better, and after he had shaved, he put on a clean shirt from his saddle bag, buckled on his gunbelt and stepped through into the parlour. There was the smell of cooking from the direction of the kitchen, making him realize just how hungry he really was. McCorg came in a few moments later. He set the rifle down in the corner near the door.

'No trouble,' he said quietly. 'If they did follow you here they must be holdin' off, probably up in the hills yonder, bidin' their time. Maybe hopin' to catch us by surprise.'

Slade regarded him in silence for a moment, then shrugged. 'When does the stage get in from the east?'

'Not for another couple of days,' said the other. 'It's a long haul over the desert with a half dozen way stations along the trail. Why the interest in the stage?'

60

'I'm just thinkin' what I would do if I was Chuck Houston. If I couldn't break the crew at the Lazy Y, could be I'd try some other way. Such as ridin' out with a few men and takin' Miss Kathy off the stage before it got here. Then I'd have the whip hand.'

McCorg's face hardened. He gazed at Slade steadily for several minutes, then said harshly, 'You figure that's what they mean to do?'

'I reckon so. Keep a few men up yonder in the hills to keep an eye on the ranch and make sure that nobody here interferes with their plans. In the meantime, Houston will ride out with the rest of his men to stop that stage.'

'Then what do we do about it?' said the other. 'I can get some of the boys together and—'

'No, that wouldn't work,' Slade said sharply. 'Any large bunch of men would be spotted without difficulty from the hills. But a small group travelling at night would have a chance of slipping through unseen.'

The foreman considered that for a moment, brow furrowed. Then he nodded in approval. 'All right, Slade. When do we start?'

'Not before dark.'

'How do you know how far Houston may have ridden back along the trail? It might not be the last stage stop where he'll attack. He may decide to get to the stage a couple of days' journey from here. He could get there ahead of us, especially if he set out last night.'

'That's a risk we'll have to take,' Slade acknowledged. 'Ain't no sense in gettin' ourselves shot to pieces.'

In the dark, it was peaceful by the small creek which ran to the north of the Lazy Y ranch. The water bubbled gently over the smooth, small-pebbled bed and there was a faint breeze whispering down from the hills, touching the tops of the trees and sighing softly in the swaying branches. Overhead, the stars shone in the velvet dome of the heavens. But the peacefulness was only an illusion and nobody knew that better than Frank Slade as he eased his mount forward along the narrow trail through the tall grass. Behind him, the other four men were moving close together in single file, making no sound as they cut through the sward and up towards the edge of the timber.

Crouching low in the saddle, Slade let his keen-eyed gaze wander over the terrain around him, watchful for the first sign of the men he knew to be somewhere in these hills. It was unlikely that they would have lit a campfire close to the timber's edge, but there was just the chance that rather than make cold, comfortless camp, they would build one deep inside the timber belt, where it would not be seen.

The first indication he had that there was anyone there was the unmistakable smell of wood smoke on the breeze that came to them through the timber. He reined his mount, held up his right hand, signalling to the others to halt. McCorg edged his horse forward until he was beside him.

'Smoke,' whispered Slade. He pointed into the trees. 'That way. They may have sentries out watching this trail. Warn the rest of the men to come forward but whatever happens, no noise! We shoot only if we're discovered.'

The Lazy Y foreman nodded, swung an arm. Slade frowned worriedly as he gigged the bay forward. The faint murmur of the stream drowned any lesser sounds, but that would not prevent them from being seen. Rounding a bend in the trail, he halted his mount suddenly. A dark figure had moved among the shadows near a clump of trees. For a moment, he could not be sure that he had actually seen a man there. The shape had vanished a moment after the faint movement had caught his attention. He knew the others had reined up and were watching him intently.

Had he been mistaken? Was it just something conjured

up by a heightened imagination. He was on the point of kneeing the bay forward again when the movement was repeated and this time he made out the winking glow of a cigarette against the gloom. Sucking in his breath, he slid from the saddle, cat-footed into the brush on the edge of the trail, moving deeper towards the undergrowth. He knew that McCorg and the others would make no move until they were certain the way was clear. With that man watching the trail from this point, it would be impossible for them to get past without being seen and a warning given even if they did manage to kill this man.

The other would have to be silenced, quickly and without noise. He did not think there would be others with him. Judging from the faint smell of cooked meat that mingled with the scent of wood smoke, they were eating their meal and would have left only the one man on watch. Easing himself forward through the undergrowth, he came up behind the man in the dark. The other's face was hidden but he had taken off his hat and had his back to Slade, leaning his shoulders against the trunk of a tree, gazing thoughtfully out over the narrow valley. Easing the heavy Colt from its holster, Slade reversed it, held it tightly by the barrel. The man straightened up while Slade was still ten feet from him and half turned, tossed the butt of the cigarette into the dirt where it flickered redly for a moment, then went out.

Slade halted for a moment, tensed himself, right hand raised. The man stepped clear of the tree, rubbed his shoulder where cramp must have been biting through it, took a single step to one side, then crashed down on to his face with only a faint murmur coming from between his lips as the butt of the Colt hit him soggily behind the ear. Bending swiftly Slade took the rifle which had fallen from the other's nerveless fingers and then moved out on to the narrow trail.

Swinging back into the saddle, he motioned the men

forward. Once they were over the brow of the hill, they were able to make better progress. Here, Slade was content to let McCorg lead the way. The other knew this country better than most, knew which trails to take to cover the greatest possible distance in the shortest time.

Dawn found them riding a trail through high rocks, a trail that ran parallel with the stage road but through higher ground so that they were able to see for several miles towards the distant horizon. As far as the eye could see, the trail was empty. The sun was not yet up, but already there was a faint red flush to the east and the stars had all paled into insignificance Although the thought that Houston might make a try for the stage had made him restless and impatient to get on, he could not shake away his natural caution. Maybe he had been wrong all along. Maybe at that very moment, Chuck Houston was back there in those trees overlooking the Lazy Y ranch, with no thought of riding out to take Kathy Curry off that stage. But with a girl's life at stake, this was one risk he could not justify taking.

They made camp on a low, rocky ridge overlooking the wide trail half an hour later. They had ridden hard during the night and every man was bone-weary although none would admit of it.

While a fire was built in a small hollow, Slade sent one of the men down to the trail to check for tracks. He was slicing the fried bacon with his knife when the man got back. The other slid from his saddle and walked over to the fire.

'Well?' said Slade tightly.

The other nodded. 'There are tracks all right,' he conceded. 'I'd say they aren't more'n a few hours old. About a dozen men, I reckon.'

'And we're only about half that number,' McCorg said gravely. He looked up at Slade.

'That's of no consequence,' the other murmured. 'We

shall have the advantage of surprise and if we can hit 'em just right, we'll have the stage driver and shotgun rider too.'

'Could be.' The other rubbed his chin, wiped the plate clean with a piece of bread. 'If they're only a few hours ahead of us, I figure they'll be makin' for the way station.'

'How far along the trail is it?'

'About eight hours ride, maybe a little more.' He nodded. 'I guess that's where the stage will put up for the night. You figure they'll wait until dark and then attack the way station?' He drew his brows together. 'That ain't likely. Once they're inside that log building, they could hold out for some time and Houston won't want to spend time in a siege.'

There was truth in what the other said. Slade nodded. 'Then they'll either take the stage just before it gets there or just after it pulls out in the morning.'

They saddled up with a renewed urgency, rode down from the overlooking hills on to the trail, the red light of the sun in their eyes.

Chuck Houston and the ten men who rode with him drew rein late that afternoon atop a long, low ridge, a saddle of ground which formed the dividing line between two wide valleys. That through which they had just ridden had been lush and green, criss-crossed by narrow, bubbling streams, but the one which faced them now, with the rays of the lowering sun slanting across it was far different. Here, the wind lifted a grey-white dust off the crests of stinging, caustic alkali and even the trail which they had followed all the way from Cross Buttes was half obliterated in places where the wind had blown the deadly dust over it. A sand lizard skittered from one of the harsh, upthrusting rocks to another, paused there for a long moment and regarded the men through unwinking agate eyes before vanishing in a blur of colour.

Houston sat high in the saddle and watched the animal race over the desert. The sorrow he had felt at the death of his brother was beginning to subside a little now, to be drowned by the surging anger and desire for revenge which had come close on its heels. Now that anger threatened to overwhelm him, to blot out every other emotion. The idea of kidnapping Kathy Curry had come to him the previous day and although, at first, he had not been certain of the advantage which having her in his hands would bring him, he had not had time in which to think things over and he knew that if he succeeded in taking her off the stage, he would have the upper hand as far as Slade was concerned. Either the other did as he was ordered, or the girl would die. It was as simple as that. Besides, he thought with a trace of grim amusement, with her in his hands, there would be no obstacle in the way of him taking over the Lazy Y ranch. Either she made it over to him and went back East, or she would simply disappear. Nothing could be simpler than that.

In spite of the heat, he was feeling somewhat pleased with himself. The fact that Slade might have figured out his intentions did not worry him in the slightest. He felt completely sure that with his men watching every way out of the Lazy Y spread, Slade and the others would have no chance whatever of following him in time to stop him from carrying through his plan.

'Reckon we got a big enough lead on anybody comin' up behind us to rest up here for a spell,' suggested the man beside him. 'The horses are tired. We are all tired. It ain't more'n another couple of hours' ride to the way station and if we're to take that stage before it gets there, we—'

'We keep on ridin',' said Houston angrily. 'I ain't underestimatin' that *hombre*, Slade. Maybe I should've shot him in town after he killed Dan. That way, we wouldn't need to do things the hard way.'

'Why didn't you, Marshal,' muttered one of the other men. 'You're the law in Cross Buttes. Leastways, if you didn't want to shoot it out with him, you could've locked him up in the jail.'

'Don't talk like a fool,' snapped Houston. Some of the anger he felt towards Slade was now directed at the men riding with him. He felt they knew he had been too scared to call Slade back in town, that he had backed down in the face of the other's threat. 'Even if Slade was killed, we would still have been forced to take care of Kathy Curry before I could have taken over the ranch. This way, it takes care of everybody. Slade won't dare to do a thing so long as we hold the girl.'

The men relapsed into silence, sat their mounts, looking without relish over the desert that stretched in front of them as far as the eye could see, out to the heat-shimmering eastern horizon. Then Houston urged his horse forward, motioning to the rest to follow. Grumbling a little, they rode out into the white, sun-baked alkali. The dust rose up in a stinging, choking cloud about them and within minutes of riding out of the rocks, they were covered by a thin, white film of dust, itching and irritating. It worked its way into the folds of their skin, where it mingled with the sweat, burning and blistering, it got between their flesh and clothing, and clogged their mouths and nostrils until it was almost impossible to breathe properly. Even when they reversed their neckpieces and drew them up over their faces, with only their eyes showing, it did little to ease their discomfort. They rode with the heat and the dust, heads lowered, eyes narrowed to mere slits.

Twelve miles further along the trail, near the eastern edge of the alkali desert, they made a wide detour, moving away from the trail itself and skirting around the way station, cutting back towards the trail, ready to meet the stage before it got to the station.

*

The stage had made good time on the run from Peco Crossing and Ben Grover had eased the team into a trot on the last run down to the way station where they would spend the night, prior to the final run through into Cross Buttes on the following day. Now he sat atop the swaying stage, holding the reins lightly between his fingers, staring off into the sunset that flamed along the horizon dead ahead of them. This was not ordinary brush country through which they were passing now that they had dropped down from the high ridges. On its fringe there were scattered clumps of mesquite and thorn, with occasional bunched masses of chapparal, interspersed by sage and prickly cactus. The trail wound along the edge of the brush since although a man could easily ride into it for a little way, it soon thickened into a veritable jungle and deeper in it was sword grass which could cut a horse's legs to ribbons. Ben Grover knew this type of country as well as anybody in the territory. He had driven this stage on its four day run from Twin Creeks for more years than he cared to remember, he knew the inhospitable miles of criss-crossing canyons and bone-dry river beds that lay in every direction on either side of the narrow, winding trail. He eased the team carefully between the walls of clawing vegetation, through the deep and strangely oppressive silence that lay over everything, over the thick, green masses. It was a nerve-tingling silence that belonged only in this place, enhanced only by the occasional sounds of the creatures of this territory; the skittering slither of a lizard as it darted from one concealing shadow to another, the quick flash of a snake on the mould-covered ground and the sharp, staccato thud of a jack rabbit.

Half a mile further on, the ground began to rise once more, becoming more rocky than before but in spite of this, there was no thinning out of the clustering vegetation. The horses were tired, a little nervous, and he tightened his grip on the reins as they flung up their heads, shying at every sudden sound.

Beside him, Brad Casson. the shotgun lying across his knees, pulled out a plug of tobacco, wrenched off a piece with a sharp twist of his strong teeth, offered the remainder to Ben.

'Thanks, Brad.' The other bit off a wad, chewed on it thoughtfully. 'Seems mighty quiet here, a little too quiet for my likin'.'

'You expectin' trouble on this run,' queried the other in mild surprise. 'We ain't haulin' anythin' on this run that anybody might be interested in.'

Ben shrugged. There had been time when they had been carrying bullion, or the payroll for some of the miners out by Cross Buttes, when he had felt this biting apprehension before. But like Brad said, there was nothing this time. A couple of passengers, both women. One had joined them at the last way station, the other, younger and prettier, had been with them all the way from the depot.

He wondered a little about her. He had not heard her name mentioned by anybody when she had joined them but he guessed she had been out East for her education and was now returning to Cross Buttes. Tall for a girl, there was a look of determination about her which led him to believe that in an argument, she would not be easily made to change her mind once it was made up. He shrugged as the thought slid through his mind. If she belonged around Cross Buttes, she might have need of just these qualities, he ruminated. From what he knew of the town, it was quickly sliding into the old ways of violence. Hardly any law there worth talking about and outlaws openly riding in, unmolested. It used to be that he felt quite at ease whenever he reached Cross buttes, during the short stay before heading back East, but no longer. It was fast becoming a hell-town in which even the decent citizens walked in fear and trembling.

A slight, but foreign sound, brought him to full alertness. Hauling sharply on the reins, he brought the team to a sliding halt.

'Somethin' wrong, old-timer?' asked Brad, leaning forward, his fingers curling around the butt of the shotgun.

'Sounds like a bunch of riders,' grunted the other. 'Not far away either and headin' in this direction.'

Brad listened intently, head cocked a little on one side, then he nodded his head slowly. 'Reckon you're right,' he conceded. He shrugged. 'Comin' up fast.' He checked the gun in his hands, threw a quick glance at the sky. Already, the flaming reds and golds in the west were beginning to fade and there was a blueness around them as the sun dropped swiftly below the horizon like a vast explosion over the distant rim of the world. 'Be dark soon.'

They sat quite still for a long moment, ascertaining the direction of the riders. Keyed to an alert tautness, Ben's ears took it all in, judging the distance of the sounds. They were coming closer all of the time, thudding hoofbeats blending with the swish and crackle of snapping branches as they cut through the trees. Soon, he was able to pick out faint voices.

He kept a tight hold on himself, knowing that the bunch of men, although still hidden, were behind them. They were still half an hour's ride from the way station and it came to him that this was a time for craft and cunning, not for blind flight. Their horses were tired from the long, dry haul over the mountain trail and their pursuers, if such they were, could easily outrun them long before they came within sight of the station.

Even as the thought crossed his mind, the tall girl thrust her head out of the stage, said sharply: 'Why have we stopped here, driver?'

'Sounds like trouble, Ma'am,' he said shortly. 'Riders comin' up fast and it's just possible they may be lookin' for us.'

'Why should they?' she demanded. There was, he noticed, no fear in her voice, merely curiosity.

'Don't ask me, Ma'am. Could be they figure we're carryin' gold, or maybe they figure that our passengers may have enough valuables on their person to make a hold-up profitable.'

'Then why aren't we making a run for it?'

'Afraid that would be of little use,' he said tightly. 'The horses are tired. We'd never make it. Besides, if we stop here we may be able to hold 'em off. They'll have to come out into the open before they can get to us and we've got the shotgun and a couple of rifles. You'd better stay inside and keep your heads down until we see what these *hombres* want.'

For a long moment, the girl looked up at him, her lips tight. Then she nodded and withdrew her head. Ben grimaced, turned to Brad. 'Better make sure that gun is loaded and ready for use.'

Over against the side of the trail was a mass of rocks, some thirty feet in height, jutting up from the ground like a row of jagged teeth. Brad motioned towards them.

'Reckon if I was to get up there, I might be able to bring some surprise fire to bear on these varmints if they do try to hold up the stage,' he affirmed.

Ben nodded, watched as the other swung himself down from the stage and ran across the trail, scrambling up into the rocks. A few moments later he had disappeared from sight and less than fifteen seconds after he had done so, the first of the riders rode into view around a bend in the trail some fifty yards behind the stationary stage.

Ben, turning in his seat, squinted back into the growing darkness, tried to make out something about the man, watched tensely as more riders appeared in the gloom.

Even his first glance was sufficient to tell him that he had been right in his first guess. These were no ordinary trail men. Neckpieces covered the lower halves of their faces and even as he caught sight of them, the leader whipped out his Colt and fired a warning shot over the stage.

'Hold it right there,' he called harshly. 'And nobody gets hurt.'

Swiftly, Ben ducked, grabbed the Winchester from its scabbard, swung the gun up and loosed off a couple of shots towards the bunch of riders, saw one of them heave himself up in his saddle, then slip sideways and hit the ground with a faint thud, lying still as his mount reared in terror about his prone body.

At the same moment, Brad opened up with the shotgun from among the rocks. The hail of shot whizzed across the clearing and the compact group of men scattered instinctively for cover, wheeling their mounts in confusion. Evidently this was the last kind of reception they had anticipated. The fact that the men riding with the stage might put up a fight seemed never to have occurred to them.

Keeping his head low, crouched down behind the rack on top of the stage, yelling a sharp warning to the two women to keep inside, Ben fired again, his lips pulled back in a snarl of defiance. A jagged pattern of gunblasts stabbed from among the brush where the gunmen had gone under cover. There came the shrill neighing of their mounts, together with shouts and curses from the men themselves.

Halting the stage and taking them from two sides had proved to be the right move in the circumstances. The enemy were still confused, had lost the advantage of surprise which they had clearly hoped to gain. Yet their position was still a highly precarious one. The hidden gunmen had only to keep them pinned down there until it was really dark and then swing around and take them from all sides. He threw a swift glance in the direction of the rocks behind which Brad lay with the shotgun. It would not be too difficult to flank that position and take the other from the rear.

The afterglow of evening was at the end of the trail but the shadows were dense on either side. One of the hidden men fired a shot and the others loosed off a barrage, the slugs hammering against the sides of the stage and ricocheting off the roof with the shrill screech of tortured metal. Ben gritted his teeth and fired three shots, spacing them into the brush. He heard one man yell loud and long and there was the unmistakable sound of a heavy body crashing among the mesquite.

Even as he fired, he tried to figure out in his own mind the reason behind this attack on the stage. It would have been a comparatively simple matter for those men out there to have discovered what he was carrying on this run and they would have no cause to try a hold-up once they knew there was no gold or valuables on board.

For a second, he saw a man's head clearly silhouetted against the skyline, drew a swift bead on it and fired. The head vanished but it was impossible for him to tell whether the slug had found its mark or not. Thumbing shells into the hot gun, he glanced down, opened his mouth to yell a warning as he saw the girl lean from the window, looking back along the trail. There was a small but deadly Derringer in her right hand. She squeezed the trigger even as one of the men darted from one side of the trail to the other. Halfway over, he stumbled, as if he had tripped over a rock, went down on his face and stayed there, unmoving.

'Nice shootin', Ma'am,' he said, unable to keep the admiration from his voice. 'But I reckon you'd better keep your head inside the stage. Those critters ain't carin' who they kill right now.'

A blast of gunfire came from the other side of the trail. Then, for a long moment, there was silence. Lying almost

73

full length behind the roof rack, Ben squinted into the growing darkness, watching for his next target and at that moment, a man's voice which he did not recognize yelled harshly: 'Better listen to me, driver. We don't have any quarrel with you or that other *hombre* up there in the rocks. As soon as it's dark, we can take you without any trouble.'

Ben called loudly: 'You're makin' a big mistake, whoever you are. We ain't carryin' gold on this trip.'

'We know that,' came the reply. 'We want one of your passengers, that's all. Turn her over to us and you'll be allowed to go on in peace. Try to stop us, and you'll all be killed.'

Ben bit his lower lip in shocked surprise. 'I only got two passengers,' he called back, 'both of 'em women. There's nobody here you want.'

'You've got Kathy Curry on that stage, mister. We want her. Like I say, turn her over to us and there'll be no more trouble.'

Ben bent his head a little. 'Either of you two ladies, Kathy Curry?' he asked in a hoarse whisper.

'Yes,' answered the younger of the two. 'I am.' There was a note of sudden puzzlement in her tone.

'You got any idea what this is all about?'

In the gloomy interior of the stage, he saw her shake her head. 'I don't know any of those men,' she declared emphatically.

'Seems to me that they sure know you.'

There was a pause, then the girl murmured: 'Are you goin' to do like they say and turn me over to them?'

Ben hesitated for only the barest fraction of a second. 'No, Ma'am,' he said tightly. 'I don't figure to know what they're after, but I ain't handin' no woman over to a bunch of coyotes like that.'

'You made up your mind yet?' shouted the hidden gunman. 'I'm not a patient man. You got ten more

74

seconds. Unless you hand her over by then, we're movin' in to take her.'

Carefully, Ben lifted the Winchester, sighted in the direction of the voice and squeezed the trigger. The heavy rifle recoiled against his shoulder and he heard the scream of the bullet whining off solid rock. 'There's your answer,' he yelled. The atrophying echoes of the shot had barely died away before a fusillade of shots rang out from the rocks and mesquite. A slug tore along Ben's arm, leaving a streak of burning pain in its wake. Brad fired another load of buckshot from the rocks above the trail. This time, Ben noticed, it came from a little nearer the outlaw's position. The blast of ear-bursting gunfire filled the air. Guns were roaring continuously now, spitting tongues of flame lancing through the gloom. Wood splintered from the rear of the stage and the team began prancing in their fear. Reaching down, he pulled on the brake as hard as he could, knowing that even this would not stop the team if they took it into their heads to bolt along the trail.

Ben rolled over to the other edge of the stage, feeling it rock and sway dangerously with the movement. He clawed at the upright, saw two of the men run from cover less than twenty yards away, racing over the open stretch of ground towards the coach. The gunfire from the rocks momentarily increased in volume as the rest of the outlaws covered their two companions. Swinging up the barrel of the rifle, he sent one shot into the nearer of the two men, saw the other throw up his arms high above his head, then fall sideways as his legs gave under him. The other man leapt over the prone body of his companion, came racing up to the coach, his Colt in his right hand. Ben squeezed the trigger of the Winchester, heard the dull, ominous click as the hammer fell on an empty breech. There was no time to roll over on to his side and tug out his pistol. The man was less than ten feet away, coming forward at a fantastic speed. Ben acted instinctively. His hand reached out for the long whip, dragged it from its place at the side of the driving box. All of his long years at handling the stage team came to the fore at that moment. Almost of its own accord, the lash of the steel tipped whip snaked through the air towards the running man. He could just make out the triumphant grin on the other's face as he sprinted for the door of the stage. The next second, the whiplash curled about his middle. Pulling with all of his strength, Ben hurled the other off his feet, arms flailing wildly as he went down. The gun in the man's hand exploded, the brief stab of flame lancing through the darkness as the bullet ploughed into the wheel of the stage.

Savagely, the man struggled to free himself, cursing wildly. He somehow managed to stagger to his feet, clawing at the lash, pulling it from around his middle. He still held his Colt in a tight-fisted grip and as he fell back once the whip was loosed from around him, he tried to bring the gun to bear on Ben. Swiftly, the other swung the whip again. This time, the lash cut across the pale blur of the man's face. He uttered a savage, shrieking yell and fell back on to his haunches as the whip drew a long line of blood across his eyes and forehead. Covering his eyes in an instinctive spasm of agony, the other rolled over and over in a blind attempt to escape the fury of that leather thong. Ben hit out again and the braided leather whistled and cracked about the man with an unholy eagerness.

In the meantime, Brad had been firing with his pistols from the cover of the rocks, trying to draw the fire of the hidden men. For a while, he was successful in this, but it soon became apparent that the outlaws were now determined to destroy the man on the stage, leaving the gunman in the rocks until later.

Thumbing shells into the Winchester, Ben searched the darkness with quick movements of his eyes. He had the feeling that the outlaws were already moving in on them from all sides. In the sudden stillness, he seemed to hear the furtive rustlings of men edging forward through the thick, tangled brush. But he could see nothing now, for it was almost completely dark. The last faint red glow in the west had been swamped by the darkness of night sweeping in from the east.

There were no more threats from the hidden men, and from his past experience, Ben knew this meant only one thing – they had no further intention of trying to scare him off, they fully intended to kill everyone there and take the girl by force. The seconds dragged themselves by on leaden feet. His ears picked out several faint sounds in the night, but his eyes could see nothing. Once or twice, he imagined he saw shadows in the brush, but whenever he swivelled his head to look directly at them, they vanished tantalisingly until he was not sure of what he had seen and he did not wish to fire until he was certain. He had very little ammunition and every bullet was precious now.

He drew up his legs, arched his back and palmed his sixgun now, breathing deep into his lungs for half a dozen breaths. He had the feeling that very soon now they would try to rush the stage, knowing that it would be impossible for him to kill them all. A second later, a solitary gunshot blew the silence into a hundred shrieking fragments. There came a second lancing tongue of flame and he saw that during the past few minutes, the outlaws had succeeded in working their way closer to the stage. Maybe if Brad were there with him, he might have been able to take a chance and whip up the team, making a run for it. These men would not dare to follow him too close to the way station. Old Gus would be waiting for them, would have become a trifle alarmed by now when they had not arrived on time. But another hour or so would elapse before he decided to ride out and take a look for them, knowing that there were several things which could cause the stage to be late: a lame horse, a thrown wheel or bad conditions out in the desert.

Another shot came to gouge a long splinter of wood out of the roof of the stage. He winced instinctively and pressed himself lower against the roof. Thrusting his hand gun over the metal bar of the rack, he fired twice, aiming blindly into the gloom, trying to pick out the lancing stilletos of flame of the muzzleblasts. More bullets hammered at the stage but before still another shot could come, he raised himself up, aimed downward and fired three times, spacing his pattern of shots so that they effectively bracketed the spot where he had seen the greatest concentration of gunshots.

Time passed again, with a short period of silence returning to the trail. Ben lay there, waiting, for what seemed an eternity, nerves pulled taut by the knowledge that there was now no way out for them, that it was only a matter of time before the outlaws moved in from every side.

'What's happening out there?' quavered the older woman from inside the stage.

'Just sit tight,' warned Ben harshly. 'If you know any prayers, I suggest you start sayin' them right now.'

Katherine Curry said firmly, but gently: 'If they only want me, I don't see any reason why the rest of you should be killed just on my account. Maybe it would be better all round if I went out there and—'

'Just you stay right where you are, Ma'am,' Ben said tightly. 'If they want you this bad, they'll shoot you down before you've gone a dozen paces.'

'But you said yourself there's nothing else we can do. If they rush us from every side, you won't be able to hold them off.'

Ben lifted his head a little. 'Quiet,' he hissed. 'I thought I heard somethin' out there.'

He strained his ears in an attempt to pick out the sound again. It had sounded like horses advancing on the trail and the hope had come to him that maybe Gus had not waited overlong once the stage failed to arrive at the way station and had taken it into his head to ride along the trail a piece and see for himself what was holding them up. Even as the thought crossed his mind, the hope died. Gus was alone back there and he could do little to help. Another gun against those which were lined up against them would make no difference whatever, apart from prolonging the inevitable for a little while.

'All right, mister,' yelled the same voice he had heard before, 'we're comin' in now. You've had your chance.'

A shadow moved in the brush. Ben fired at it instinctively, saw it melt away into the background darkness. More gunblasts blossomed out from the brush, he heard the hum of bullets passing close to his head as he flung himself down. Then there came another sharp volley of gunfire that made him cringe as he lay there. Seconds passed before the realisation came to him that the gunfire was not directed at the stage but into the brush on either side of the trail.

FOUR

BUZZARD TRAIL

Swinging abruptly from the saddle, Slade fired on the run, cut down one man who tried to dive for cover. The others, he guessed, were among the sage and chapparal which bordered the trail. Swiftly, he motioned to McCorg and the rest of the men to spread out, saw them move in, then crouched down behind a deadfall, just able to make out the shape of the stage thirty yards away in the middle of the trail. The driver was still alive. He saw the man's gun bloom crimson fire as he opened up on the men in the tall grass. There was no sign of the man who had been riding shotgun, but a few seconds later, he saw a Colt lance flame into the darkness from a clump of rocks on the opposite side of the trail and reckoned it was highly likely that the man had succeeded in climbing up there into a vantage point before Houston and his men had attacked.

Vaguely silhouetted in the gloom, he saw a small knot of horses, guessed that Houston had ordered his men to advance on foot when they had reached the stage. If he could spook those mounts, there was a good chance of forcing a showdown with Houston right here and now, he reflected. But his chance of doing this was thwarted a moment later as a bunch of men broke from cover and began running back to the tethered mounts. Swiftly, he threw lead at them as they crashed among the stunted trees, saw one man stumble, lurch and then go down. A moment later, the wounded man somehow staggered to his feet and continued forward after the others, yelling loudly in a shrill voice.

McCorg came running up out of the gloom, his breath harsh in his lungs.

Slade pointed. 'There they go,' he said hoarsely. He fired again at the men as they struggled to untether their mounts and saddle up. One man, a knife in his hand, bent and slashed savagely, frenziedly, at the rope which tied his horse to the bole of a tree. The rope parted and the hammer clicked dully on a spent cartridge in Slade's gun. Angrily, knowing there was no time to reload now, he thrust it back into leather, straightened up. In a tight bunch, Houston and his men rode back along the trail, heads low as they passed beneath the overhanging branches of the trees. The sound of their hoofbeats faded swiftly into the distance.

Slade paused long enough to make sure it was safe to step out into the open, then walked towards the stage. The driver, a grizzled oldster, lifted himself a little sheepishly from his position on the roof, dusted himself down and said grumpily, 'Thanks, mister. I reckoned we were all buzzard meat until you showed up. How'd you happen to be along like that?'

'Weren't an accident,' said McCorg, nodding to the other. 'We've been trailin' those coyotes all day.'

'Then you knew they meant to hold up the stage?' said the other incredulously.

'Let's say we figured they might,' Slade said. He stepped forward and opened the door, looking inside. He saw the frightened face of the woman crouched in the far corner and smiled reassuringly. 'Everything is all right now, Ma'am,' he told her. 'We'll soon have you at the way station.'

Before he could say anything further, the girl nearest the door said in a spirited voice: 'And why aren't you riding after those murderers?'

Slade smiled. The girl stepped down on to the trail. She was tall, taller than he had expected, came higher than his shoulder, slender but with a supple strength. She held her head high as she stared at him.

'Katherine Curry,' he said softly. For a moment he was nonplussed. He had last seen her as a young girl with her hair in braids. He had never dreamed that she would have turned out to be as beautiful and composed a woman as this. There was certainly a lot of her father's spirit in her.

'That is my name,' she replied. Her brows were drawn together in puzzlement. 'But how do you know it?' A sharper tone entered her voice as she went on quickly: 'Or are you in with that gang who tried to hold us up? They wanted me for some reason and—'

'I think I can explain everything on the way to the station,' he told her quietly. 'You see, I sent that telegram asking you to come home at once.'

He saw her expression change, soften a little, her lips curving into a smile. 'So you're Frank Slade. Father often talks about you, about the old days. I'm glad to meet you again. You haven't changed much over the past few years.'

She held out her hand to him, her grip firm and friendly. Helping her back into the stage, he climbed in beside her, handing the reins of his mount to McCorg.

A few minutes later, once Brad had joined them, they started off again, the coach bumping and swaying precariously from one side of the trail to the other.

'Now,' said Kathy quietly, 'suppose you tell me what all this is about. I never expected a welcome like this. Who were those men back there and what did they want with me?'

Slade bit his lip momentarily. This was the part he had dreaded. He had deliberately refrained from mentioning her father's death in the telegram, believing it would be far better to tell her in person when they met; but at the time, he had never thought it would be under conditions such as this.

'I'm afraid I have some very bad news for you, Kathy. I only wish we could have met in happier circumstances.'

He saw her face change in the gloom, saw the sudden tightening of her lips, knew that she had half guessed what it was he had to say, yet she remained silent, afraid, waiting for him to speak the words.

'It's about your father, Kathy,' he went on slowly, hesitantly.

'He's dead. That's what you're trying to tell me, isn't it?' There was no emotion in her voice, no expression whatsoever.

'Yes. It happened before I rode into town. I was on my way to see him when I met McCorg, the foreman and the rest of the crew. They were for ridin' out and leaving the place, but I persuaded them to ride back with me and wait until you came back and decided what to do with the ranch.'

He watched the way her mouth struggled to hold its firm shape, saw her bottom lip begin to quiver, the tears come unbidden to her eyes. She wanted to cry, but something within her held her back. He felt her body tremble against his.

She swallowed, then said hoarsely: 'How did it happen? How did he die, Frank?'

'I don't know all of the details. Only what I picked up in town but—' He paused, unsure of how to go on, knowing that he would have to tell her the truth and that it would wreak its misery in her and be hard to bear, but that there was nothing else he could do, no way he could possibly soften the blow.

'Please tell me,' she said quietly, forcing evenness into her voice, not allowing herself to let go. 'I'd rather hear it from you.'

'Houston, the Town Marshal, took your father into town on a charge of rustlin'. The charge was made by Cal Weston, your neighbour.'

'Weston?' She looked at him in surprise. 'But I thought he was Dad's friend. Why should he bring a charge like that against him?'

'I'm not sure. I suspect that Houston paid him to do so. But anyway, he was locked up in the town jail to await the arrival of the circuit judge in a few weeks' time. Sometime during the night, Weston and some of his cronies got a lynchin' party together and shortly after dawn went along to the jail and forced Houston to turn your father over to them. They took him along to the saloon and carried out a mock trial at which he was found guilty of the charge. Then they took him out and hung him.'

He heard her sharp intake of breath, her mouth open as she lifted her head to stare up at him. Some tears ran down her cheeks and fell warmly on his hand. She showed him an expression that meant nothing to him, her gaze stony. He knew that she wanted to hate the world, to blame everybody for what had happened. When the news really sank into her numbed mind, when the shock wore off, it would be even worse.

'But why?' she asked finally. 'Why should this happen to him?'

Slade put out his hand and covered hers, gripping the fingers tightly. 'I think I know,' he said slowly. 'Houston was at the back of it all. He and his brother Dan wanted to rule the territory as well as the town. But your father stood in their way. He warned his men not to go near the town, then threatened to get rid of Houston by force if he had to, warning the townsfolk what sort of men these two brothers were. So he paid Weston to make this charge and got him to get the lynchin' party together.'

'But have you any proof of this?'

'Some. The fact that Houston planned to hold up the

stage and take you off it is the best proof. They probably meant to use you to force my hand.'

'But why have you been brought into it?'

'I went into town and called out Dan Houston, forced a showdown with him. He tried to bushwhack me, but he wasn't quick enough. I shot him down in the street and now Chuck Houston, the Town Marshal, has sworn to kill me. He figured that with you in his hands, he could force me to give myself up, and then he would make you sell him the Lazy Y ranch.'

'That I'll never do,' she said tautly. 'If what you say is true and he was the man who arranged Dad's death, then I won't rest until he's been paid in full.'

There was no time for further conversation. The stage drew up with a squeal of brakes in front of the way station and while McCorg and the others took their mounts over to the corral, the others went inside, into the warmth and the light. Food had been prepared for them and Gus, his white beard fanning over his chest, beamed at them in the yellow glow from the lanterns swinging from the low beams.

Not until the meal was finished and Slade was standing in the shadows outside the building, careful not to expose himself in the beam of yellow light which spilled through the open doorway, did he turn to find Kathy Curry .standing quietly beside him. She stared out into the night in silence for a long moment before speaking.

'You were a great friend of my father's, Frank,' she said softly. 'I want you to help me now.'

'I'll do anythin' I can, Miss Kathy. You know that.'

'I'm glad. Until tonight, I thought everything was going to be fine. I'd come back, maybe help Dad on the ranch. But it isn't going to be like that. This is a hard and cruel country and I have to be hard so that I can face it. It isn't going to be easy for me, not to begin with, anyway. Do you think the rest of the crew will stay on, will work under a woman?'

'If they won't, both McCorg and I will want to know the reason why,' he said.

She gave him a keen glance, suddenly arrested by the remark. He knew that she wanted to trust him, knew that she had to trust him, because there was no one else to whom she could turn at that moment. 'It isn't easy to realize that he's gone,' she went on, her voice a low murmur, almost lost in the other night sounds. 'It isn't until you lose someone like him that you realize how much you came to rely on him, on his strength, on the decisions he made and the orders he gave. It's going to be an empty, lonely place without him. That's why I want you to take over and help me run the ranch.'

Slade paused at that. He said slowly, deliberately: 'Now hold hard there, Miss Kathy. Sure I was your father's friend and I want to help you all I can, but as to staying on at the ranch, that's a horse of a different colour. I don't see that I can stay indefinitely.'

She studied his face for a moment in the dimness, trying to read what she saw there, but unable to do so. 'Is this a way of saying that you can't help me?'

'No, it's not that. But I have a chore to do and—'

'You mean to see that Chuck Houston doesn't kill you, or that you intend to kill him?' For a second there was open dislike in her voice, then she reached out and touched his arm. 'I'm sorry. I oughtn't to have said that. I've got no right to ask you to give up everything to stay here in Cross Buttes and help me.'

'You've got every right,' he said slowly. 'Even if only because your father saved my life on two occasions. But once you've settled in, you'll not need me, or anyone else. There's a lot of your father in you, Kathy. You know what you want and you go right ahead and get it, no matter what it costs.'

'I know what I want right now,' she said slowly, solemnly. 'To avenge my father's brutal and wanton murder and then to turn the ranch into what my father would have wanted it to be if he were still alive. Surely that isn't too much to want. I know I sound hard and cruel, but that's how I will have to be until this job is finished.' Her lips were pressed tightly together, eyes narrowed a little. In a flat, emotionless voice, she went on: 'Houston is going to find that he made the worst mistake of his life when he failed to take me prisoner tonight.'

Looking at her in the gloom, Slade found it impossible not to believe her. This was not the girl he had once known, happy and carefree. The events of the past few days had wrought a great change in her, had wiped out all of those happy memories, and replaced them by a deep and terrible need for revenge.

He said: 'I don't like to see such hardness in a woman, even under circumstances such as these. You have every right to feel angry and bitter, but leave this chore to men.'

She turned to face him and when she spoke again, it was as if she had never heard him. 'Do you think those killers are still around, that they may try to attack us here, tonight?'

'It's possible, but unlikely. Houston lost a lot of his men when he tried to attack the stage. Somehow, I doubt if the others will have the stomach for any more fightin'. No, they'll have ridden on back to Cross Buttes where, no doubt, he'll be thinkin' up some other plan to destroy you.'

Shortly before noon the next day, the stage rolled down the main street of Cross Buttes, with Ben seated on the driver's platform, the reins held tightly in his fists, Brad sitting up beside him, shotgun cradled in the crook of his arm. The journey from the final way station had proved to be uneventful. There had been nothing but the dust and the leaping jack rabbits to keep them company.

Inside the stage, Slade sat beside Kathy Curry, keeping

a watchful eye on the scene outside. There might be trouble in the town, and he had detailed McCorg and the others to ride in with them, just in case Houston decided to try his luck again. But there was no sign of the burly marshal as the stage rolled forward in its own cloud of dust, to halt in front of the depot. Slade alighted and helped the two ladies down, glanced up at Ben Grover.

'Better stable the horses, Ben,' he called, 'then get that wound on your arm attended to.'

'Ain't nothin' but a scratch,' demurred the other. He swung himself down with an agility that belied his years.

Turning to the girl, Slade said: 'It isn't safe for you to stay here in town any longer than necessary. Out at the ranch, you will be far safer.'

She nodded. He noticed that her eyes were wider and darker than before. Then she nodded. 'I can get a buckboard at the livery stable,' she told him. 'Perhaps you would drive me back.'

'Of course.' He took her arm, led her along the boardwalk in the direction of the livery stable. As he walked, his keen eyes switched from one side of the street to the other, wary and alert. It was not until they were only a few yards from the stables that there was any sign of trouble. A man stepped down from the boardwalk on the opposite side of the street, angled across, his spurs raking up the dust underfoot. Slade's eyes swung to the other instantly and his right hand moved just an inch to hover close to the gunbutt at his side. He did not know the other, but there was the feel of danger in the air and also in the way the other folk on the street seemed to melt back into the shadows.

'I want to talk to you, Slade,' called the other harshly. 'I want to see what a gunslinger looks like.'

Slade was aware of the girl's sharp intake of breath as it hissed through tightly clenched teeth. He felt her body tense next to his.

'Cal Weston,' she said. There was venom in her voice. 'I thought you were my father's friend, but instead you became his murderer.'

'Your father rustled my best beef,' Weston said harshly, not taking his eyes off Slade's face for a single instant as he spoke. 'All I did was see that the sentence was carried out. But this gun-totin' *hombre* here shot down Dan Houston in cold blood. I saw it with my own eyes.'

'You're a liar, Weston,' Slade said sharply. 'And a cold-blooded murderer. If you want to call me out, go right ahead.'

The other grinned viciously, kept his hands swinging well clear of his guns. 'I don't aim to draw against you, Slade,' he said thinly. 'I've heard of your reputation as a killer and I don't figure on givin' you the satisfaction of shootin' me down like you did Dan. But I'll do it with my bare hands unless you're too much of a coward to face up to me.' As he spoke, he unbuckled his gunbelt and tossed it away from him to land with a soft thud in the dust.

He stood waiting in a half crouch, eyes fixed on Slade's face. Very slowly, knowing that the eyes of the crowd were on him, Slade unfastened his own belt and let it drop at his feet, moving forward. He heard the girl say tightly: 'Be careful, Frank. Don't trust him.'

Taking a step forward, he moved into the street. In the same instant, the other rushed forward, arms swinging wildly. Slade waited for him to come on, side-stepped swiftly and hit the other a sharp jabbing blow on the side of the head as his momentum carried him blindly forward. Weston bellowed loudly as he staggered under the force of the blow, but managed to stay on his feet. He spun quickly, sucking in great draughts of air, his chest heaving. His eyes were narrowed to mere slits and he moved around Slade, manoeuvring the other so that he was facing into the glaring light of the sun. Slade blinked. For a moment he was temporarily blinded and cursed himself for his folly in not seeing what the other had in mind. A blow caught him on the side of the face, made his head ring. He felt the salty taste of blood on his lower lip, backed away as the other continued forward. But Weston's rash impetuousness proved to be his undoing. His belief that he had Slade licked from the very beginning was his downfall. As he moved in, hammering short, sharp blows at the other's ribs, he left himself wide open. Swaying his head to one side, Slade steadied himself, hit the other flush on the nose, felt a solid satisfaction as he felt the cartilege go under his knuckles.

Gasping on the blood that ran into his throat, Weston gave ground until he had his back to the wooden rail along the edge of the boardwalk. His face was puffed and bloody and his breath was coming in short, hard gasps that threatened to tear his chest in two. But there was still plenty of fight left in him, he was far from beaten. Dazedly, he swung a couple of wild, haymakers at Slade and by sheer luck, one of them connected. It crashed into Slade's chest, almost caving in his ribs by the sheer force of it. For a moment, he was almost completely paralysed, scarcely able to draw a breath, a red mist dancing in front of his vision. Had it not been for the fact that the other was in almost as bad a state as he was at that moment, the fight might have been ended there and then, but Weston was still gasping for air, swaying drunkenly on his feet as Slade fought to regain his senses. Through the mist that hovered in front of him, he saw the other moving forward, squaring up, his face a snarling, bloody mask of savage anger.

Shaking his head in an attempt to clear it, he moved to one side, felt a hard fist crash into his side, but scarcely felt it now. His body seemed to possess a surface numbness such as a fighter gets during a long, hard fight. Slowly, he felt the strength begin to flow back into his body as his lungs sucked in the dusty air and his head cleared. He was able to make out the other again. The street and buildings ceased their whirling gyrations around him. He felt his legs steady as he braced himself to meet the other's forward rush.

Weston tried to bring up his knee, to hit the other in the groin, but Slade had outguessed him, was expecting the move. Backing swiftly, he reached out and clamped a tight hold around the other's leg, heaved with all of his strength. Weston gave a wild yell of fear and pain and went over backwards, landing with a heavy thump in the dust. For a moment he lay there, almost knocked out by the bone-jarring impact. Then his right hand moved, not to push himself up on to his feet, but snaking inside his jacket, reaching for the hidden gun in the shoulder holster.

Quickly, almost without thinking, Slade stepped forward, brought his heel down hard on the other's wrist as he withdrew the gun from inside the jacket. He bore his full weight down on the other, the sharp heel of the boot grinding into flesh and bone with a relentless pressure. Weston let out a piercing yell, tried to haul his wrist free and wriggle away. Seeing this was impossible, he rolled hard against Slade's knees, hoping to throw him off balance, but Slade dropped his knees straight on to the other's ribs, heard the breath go out of him with a sudden whoosh, seized the gun and tossed it away, then rose back, waiting.

Grunting with the effort, Weston staggered to his feet. He had made his play and used his last trump card, and lost. Now there was the look of a trapped animal on his face, lips drawn back over his teeth in a snarling smile. His arms hung feebly by his sides, as if he lacked the strength to lift them. Over the other's shoulder, Slade caught a glimpse of Houston, standing on the edge of the board-walk a short distance away, watching what was going on with interest. There, however, something in the other's taut attitude which puzzled him for a long moment until, out of the corner of his eye, he saw McCorg, seated on his mount, a few yards away, his sixgun levelled on the other, watching his every move. The rest of the onlookers would not interfere, Slade knew; they were the kind who had long ago learned never to butt into another man's business unless it directly concerned themselves. They were probably enjoying the fight.

Slowly, Weston came forward in a bent-over crouch. Then he made a sudden, unexpected spring from the waist, seemed to jack-knife forward, arms opening wider, evidently seeking to get a grip around Slade's waist and bear him backward so that he could bring his weight advantage to bear. Slade waited patiently for him to come on, then brought up his knee sharply, aiming it for the other's bent head. There was a sharp, ominous crack as it struck the other on the point of the chin, jerking his head back like that of a puppet on a string. Weston uttered a strangled gasp and dropped on to his knees, his arms falling away. He held himself painfully on his hands and knees, sucking in great lungfuls of air, struggling to remain conscious. He was shaking his head ponderously from side to side, scarcely knowing where he was or what had happened to him. Very slowly, an inch at a time, he lifted his head, stared about him blankly for a long moment, then fixed his gaze on Slade's face as the other stood over him. Swaying, he tried desperately to pull himself upright, was on his knees when the side of Slade's hand, swinging downward, struck him with a bone-shaking force on the back of the neck. It was the *coup-de-grace* as far as the other was concerned. Weston pitched forward on to his face, arms and legs outflung, and stayed there, unmoving. A weaker neck would have broken under the shattering impact of that blow. As it was, the other would be out for a long while. Slade stepped back from the unconscious man, lifted his head and glared at Houston.

'I reckon he ought to be glad I didn't kill him,' he said

through his teeth. 'If he gets in my way again, I will.'

Houston flushed, held his temper in check with a tremendous effort, switching his gaze from Slade to McCorg. 'You're talkin' very brave so long as that man of yours holds a gun down on me,' he grated thickly. His eyes were slitted, his body pressed forward, it seemed involuntarily, as if he would throw himself across the street at the other.

'Don't provoke me, Houston,' Slade said thinly. 'I know it was you led those men in the hold-up attempt on the stage yesterday. No doubt you've got men here who'll swear how you was in town all that time, but you don't fool me. As soon as I can prove it, I'll come ridin' back into town to see that justice is done. In the meantime, my warnin' to you is stay away from the Lazy Y ranch.'

Houston's eyes took on a crafty expression. 'I always like to get orders like that from the owner,' he said softly. He bowed slightly in Kathy Curry's direction. 'I'm only sorry we have to meet like this, Miss Curry,' he said disarmingly. 'Those men who lynched your Dad were actin' outside of the law.'

'Then why did you do nothing to stop them?' asked the girl in an icy tone.

Houston shrugged. 'They had guns on me, Ma'am and there were close on a dozen men. What chance would I have had against that mob. Somebody stirred 'em up and when I find out who it was, I'll—'

'This is one of the murderin' curs who did it,' Slade snapped, jabbing the toe of his boot into Weston's ribs. 'Accordin' to the rumours goin' around, he was the leader of that mob, the *hombre* who pulled the rope.'

'You got no proof of that, Slade,' gritted the other. 'And the fact that you've already committed one murder in Cross Buttes makes you no better even if what you say happens to be true.'

'I'll get the proof,' Slade said. 'When I do, I'll come

gunnin' for you both. Just chew that up a bit, Houston.'

Houston's face was white, showing up with vivid red blotches, his eyes glittering with rage. For a moment, the thought of action was in his eyes, even with McCorg's gun levelled on him. Then he stepped back a pace on to the boardwalk. 'It ain't wise to threaten the law, Slade, as you'll find out to your cost.' He turned his attention back to Kathy Curry. 'Whatever quarrel I've got with this man, Miss Curry, has nothin' to do with the business between you and me. With your father dead, you'll find it difficult, if not impossible, to run the ranch. If you ever think of sellin' out, I'll be only too glad to make you a handsome offer. Think it over before you make up your mind. This is no country for a young woman such as yourself. There are evil ways here that you do not understand, forces which could destroy you. My advice is to go back East where you really belong, forget this place and all of its memories.'

Kathy Curry drew herself up to her full height. There was something close to naked scorn in the eyes she turned on him. 'I intend to run the ranch just as my father did,' she told him. 'I may even change a few things. He was a little too trusting of people around him.' Here, her gaze fell for a moment on the unconscious figure of Cal Weston lying in the dust in the middle of the street, 'but I'm a little more careful about who I call my friend.'

Slade watched Houston grow cold, grow keen. A new expression came on to his mottled features. Then he nodded his head slowly, decisively, as if he had just made up his mind about something important.

'I only hope that your trust is never misplaced,' he said harshly. Abruptly, he turned on his heel and walked back to the sheriff's office, slamming the door behind him.

Slade turned to the men crowding around him. He could feel a little trickle of blood on his cheek and put up the back of his hand to it. Harshly, he said: 'Better toss a bucket of water on to him, boys. See that he doesn't try to ride out after me, or they'll be bringin' him back across a buckboard.'

Taking Kathy's arm, he walked with her to the livery stables. Here they hired a buckboard and drove out of town in the direction of the ranch. McCorg and the others rode a little way behind them, watchful for any pursuit, but only their own dust cloud hung in the air around them.

Consciousness for Cal Weston was ushered in by an insistent throbbing in his head, a throbbing pain that became more and more intense and agonising as his mind cleared. He shook his head, winced at the pain that lanced through it, was aware of the water that lay on his face, running into his eyes, half blinding him as he forced them to stay open. With an effort, he sucked air down into his lungs, struggled to sit up, clenching his teeth against the agony. Daylight shone directly into his eyes and vaguely he was aware of the men standing over him. His jaw hurt and there was a dull ache in his chest as if several of his ribs had been bruised or broken. A hand reached down, grabbed him beneath the elbow and jerked him none too gently to his feet, holding him there as he swayed and would have fallen but for the other's restraining grip on him.

Weston saw then that the marshal and some of the other men were standing near him, that he had been lying in the middle of the street. He put up a hand and rubbed the back of his neck. Most of the pain seemed to be centred there and memory returned with a rush. That slugging match with Slade. He winced at the sharp pain which even his light touch evoked. His legs barely supported his weight but with a savage, angry gesture, he pulled his arm away from the supporting grasp, managed to stand on his own two feet.

'Where the hell is Slade?' he asked through swollen lips.

'He's pulled out of town,' Houston said in a vaguely sneering tone. 'I thought you had it in you to fix him. Seems I've been wrong about you all the way, Weston.'

The other rubbed his mouth with the back of his hand, stared down for a moment at the blood smeared across his fingers. Then he said thinly: 'What the hell is that supposed to mean, Houston? I did everythin' you asked of me. I saw to it that Curry was removed permanently. If you're so goddamned disapproving, why didn't you do your own dirty work?'

'All right, all right,' said the other quickly. 'So you do have your uses. But we've got to stop Slade from spoilin' our plans. Seems he's talked the girl into holdin' on to the ranch. She's more'n likely as stubborn as the old man was and, if so, we'll not get her to sell out easily.'

'There are more ways than one of forcin' her hand,' Weston said savagely. 'I figure I've got a score to settle with Slade too.'

Houston looked at him sharply. 'Slade is mine,' he said warningly. 'He shot Dan and for that, I mean to kill him. But slowly and in my own good time. If you want revenge, then you'll bring him in alive. Leave the rest to me.'

Weston contemplated the other for a long moment, then nodded his head slowly. 'All right, if that's the way you want it. But I want to be there when he gets it.'

'Come over to the office,' Houston said. 'We've got to plan this carefully. Reckon we can't afford any more mistakes.'

'If you'd stopped that stage and got the girl last night, we wouldn't have to plan anythin' more,' Weston said tightly, as he fell into step beside the other. 'Slade would have been forced to do anythin' we said.'

Houston paused outside the door of the sheriff's office. 'Don't blame me for that fiasco last night,' he said tautly. 'I left you with the others to watch the Lazy Y ranch, to stop any of 'em from ridin' out. Seems to me that you

96

didn't do that chore very well. Somehow, Slade and those others got through and took us by surprise.'

'That was Secomb's fault,' Weston retorted. 'He let 'em through.'

'Let's stop tryin' to pass the blame for this,' said one of the other men. ' We've got to make sure the next time.'

Houston went over to the desk and leaned on it, saying nothing, staring from one man to the other. After a while, he opened his tobacco sack and built himself a smoke, curling the cigarette slowly in his fingers. Weston and the three other men in the office watched him light up, inhale, exhale, then twist from the waist to stare at them closely. 'Any of you got any ideas?' he asked sharply.

It was Weston who spoke first, fingering his jaw tenderly, his eyes bright with an inner anger. 'I can muster a score of men who'll ride with me any time I give the word,' he affirmed. 'I say we ought to ride out to the Lazy Y after dark and put the place to the torch.'

'You figure there's a chance of doin' that?' queried Houston, sucking in his cheeks reflectively. 'They'll be expectin' an attack and they could be lyin' in wait for us. We'd lose a heap of men if we ran into their defences.'

'They won't be reckonin' on us ridin' out there tonight,' said the other tautly. 'There's an old Indian trail over the hills we could take. If we rode hard, we could be at the Lazy Y shortly after sundown.'

'You sure of this?' Houston sat bolt upright on the edge of the desk.

'Of course I'm sure.'

'Then what are we waitin' for? Get your men together and we'll ride out.' His teeth snapped together as the thought of finishing both Slade and the girl came to him.

Not more than twenty minutes later, a score of men, hard-faced and tight-lipped, rode out of town. The dust of their passing settled slowly and behind them, Cross Buttes settled down into the quietness of late afternoon. Leaving town, they pushed on uptrail, with Weston in the lead, rising with the short switchback courses of the lower hills, climbing steeply with every mile along the edge of the razor-backed ridges. The land that stretched away in front of them proved to be extremely deceptive. There were long stretches where it was almost level, running on beside some swift-flowing stream, the air thick and damp and cold. Further on, they cut up into the rocks. In places, it was almost impossible to make out the trail at all and as he rode behind Weston, Houston felt the urge to move even more quickly than they were at the moment, but he held the sensation down. He knew none of this land, yet even so he felt no real concern as he let his glance wander over the massive, fantastic buttes and mesas which lay around them in every direction. They were high above the valley now and the town was somewhere far behind them along the trail, out of sight. By degrees, the country roughened, the going proved more difficult. He began to doubt Weston's belief that they could reach the Lazy Y ranch by nightfall.

Crossing the crest of the high hills, they made their way downgrade, now riding in the shadow of the great peaks. Here, it was a deep blue world of dim first-growth pine, massive at the butt and rising in flawless symmetry to the overhead mat of branches and leaves. The trees ran solemnly before them as they followed Weston in single file. Beneath the arch of boughs, it was difficult to tell whether the sun had already set or not but gradually, the pines became smaller, more stunted and the rocky ravines came down towards them, hemming them in on both sides. They crossed the wide shoulder of the hills and halfway along the trail, Weston held up his right hand and halted the file of men.

'What is it?' Houston demanded sharply. 'Why have we stopped here?'

'The perimeter of the Lazy Y spread is down yonder,

just around the bend in the trail,' Weston answered shortly. 'If we go blunderin' along as we are, we could easily bump into one of their line camps and that could be disastrous.'

'All right. We'll keep our eyes open. But keep movin'.'

There was water flowing at the bottom of the slide. They forded the river, putting their mounts into the strong current, raced them up the far bank and came out of the rocks near the rim of the rolling grasslands. The abrupt change in the character of the country took Houston by surprise.

Far away there came the faint lowing of cattle and, turning in the saddle, he peered out into the growing darkness, was just able to make out the darker shadow of the herd on the lower slopes of the hills on the far edge of the valley. He nodded to Weston. 'Looks as though they have their camp yonder. They won't worry us.'

Considering this, Weston nodded, kicked his mount, urged it forward across the valley. He had his mind entirely on this business and still, from time to time, the thought that perhaps he had been wrong, that Slade would not wait to warn the crew of the Lazy Y once he got there, and there would be men lying in wait for them, kept coming back to worry him. And then other thoughts moved through his head in rapid succession. Slade would not be expecting any trouble so soon. He would believe that Houston would stay in town until he was able to think out some plan and it was certain that Slade did not know of that trail over the hills, would not believe it possible for anybody to reach the ranch in less than four or five hours.

The thought made him easier in his mind. Keeping well away from the middle of the valley where they would be easily seen even in the darkening gloom, they skirted around the rim. Their way lay upgrade for a mile or more, with the land on their right gradually growing less rough; afterwards, the trail turned and dipped sharply, moved past a line of timber, growing tall and straight, then the trail widened and became broader, better.

Now it was Houston who felt the need for caution. He rode up beside Weston and said harshly: 'How far are we from the ranchhouse?'

'About a mile,' replied the other. He pointed. 'Just beyond the ridge yonder. Those trees ought to hide us from anybody down there until we're ready to move in.'

'Good. But we move slow now. We don't want to be anywhere near the trail from town when Slade and the others come along it. I want to wait until it's completely dark before we go in.'

'All right. Just so long as we don't wait too long.' The other rubbed his bruised cheek meaningly.

'We'll wait just as long as I say,' snapped Houston angrily. 'I'm runnin' this show, not you.'

Weston sat straight in his saddle. There was an ugly look on his face as he faced the other. 'These are my men ridin' with us,' he reminded the marshal. 'I don't see you havin' brought along anyone except for yourself, and then only because you want to be in at the kill, you want to be sure that I don't kill Slade and rob you of your revenge.'

Houston sucked in his breath sharply. For a moment, his right hand was lifted close to the butt of his gun, then he let it fall, shoulders shrugging a little. 'All right, Weston. So these are your men. But if we start by fightin' now, we don't have a chance of gettin' either Slade or the girl.'

'Some riders headin' along the trail yonder,' said one of the other men a few feet away. His voice sounded queerly excited and nervous.

Houston's hands became knotted fists as he peered off into the distance, pushing his sight through the darkness. The dust cloud showed first and then he was able to make out the shape of the buckboard and the small group of men riding close behind it. He turned his attention back to the men with him, eyeing them with a swift, sharpened interest.

'Looks like you were right, Weston,' he said grudgingly. 'Now we wait for full dark and then move in.'

'Why not hit 'em now?' asked Weston.

Houston shook his head. 'We'll wait for a while. No sense in pushin' our luck too far.'

They sat in silence, each man with his own thoughts. The foothills and the brush country faded and there were only the yellow lights visible, streaming out through the windows of the ranchhouse, less than a mile away.

FIVE

NIGHT ATTACK

Taking off his shirt, Slade filled the washbowl in the corner of the room from the tall pitcher and when he washed, he felt the water sting his face, felt the mask of dust and alkali crack on his skin. It had been a long drive out from the town and most of the way the air had been hot and filled with dust. His cheeks and jaw ached from the fight with Cal Weston and there was a cut on his lower lip where his teeth had been driven into it.

Shaking the dust from his shirt, he put it back on, went over to the window and stared out into the night. Kathy Curry had insisted that as long as he stayed at the ranch, he was to occupy this rear room which had been her father's. The rest of the men, he knew, were now in the bunkhouse and all around the ranchhouse, everything was still and quiet, the silence broken only by the distant wail of a prairie dog or the movement of the horses in the corral.

Upending the water pitcher, he drank all he could hold, then set it down again to the bowl. As he stood there he contemplated the events of the past few days, tried to figure out what Houston and Weston intended to do now that their hand had been forced back there in Cross Buttes. Weston still had several men he could call on in the event of a showdown. Whether he would threw in his lot with Chuck Houston was, of course, another matter. He might have decided that he had had enough of this range war, that things were getting a little too hot for him to handle and if Houston wanted to go on with this vendetta, then he would have to go it alone.

Maybe if he had not fought him and given him that hiding in the main street of town that was what he would undoubtedly have done. But the fact that he had been beaten up like that, and in front of Houston and the townsfolk, would certainly weigh heavily in any decision he might make.

Reaching forward, he opened the window and let the scent and the sounds of the night come in. The energy of his supper had acted as a stimulant which made him forget the weariness that had been in his body during the long drive back from town, through the oppressive heat and dust of the afternoon. He felt oddly restless and apprehensive. It was a feeling he did not like, but also one he could not throw off.

Kathy Curry had taken the shock of her father's death extremely well. She had borne herself with a quiet dignity which had made a profound impression on him. He did not doubt that soon, once the initial shock had worn off, the tears would come and it would be a great help if she would surrender herself to them. At heart, she was not really the cold and independent person she tried to appear. At that moment, perhaps, she was in her room, weeping for her father, for the days which were gone and which could never return. There was a sudden feeling of helplessness bubbling within him. He could avenge her father's death if that was what she really wanted, deep down inside, he could use his gun to protect her and her ranch; but he could do and say little which would be of real comfort to her in this time of her grief.

Strangely, he felt himself drawn to her. His last memory

103

of her had been of a young girl, barely in her teens, anxious to ride the most fickle mounts on the ranch, determined to help around the place, not wanting to go out East to become a lady, pleading with her father to allow her to remain there, to grow up and become a part of the West. But in the end, his will had triumphed and, tearful, she had gone. He sighed as he recalled the days of long ago. It was not easy to believe that so many years had passed since then, that events had changed them both, so that at first, when they had met, they had almost not recognized each other.

Building himself a smoke, he leaned against the wall beside the window. For the first time in several days, he remembered the real reason why he was here in this part of the territory. He had a job to do and although he would naturally do all he could to help Kathy, he still had this other chore to do for the State Governor. One of the Houston brothers was dead, but the other, perhaps potentially the more dangerous of the two, was still alive. And where was Chuck Houston at that moment? It was something he would have dearly liked to know.

He had no need of the cigarette which he had made and held it unlit between his lips for a long moment in his idleness as he looked over over the ground outside the ranch house. A man moved out of the bunkhouse, his body alternately visible as he passed through the beams of lamplight that poured through the windows further along the house. Slade watched him with a part of his attention.

Then he lifted his glance, looked beyond the other, thinking how beautiful this place could be. It needed only a man to manage it and several good years in the territory when the cattle fattened in peace. The trouble in the past had been that too often there were bad years also, when the smell of gunpowder hung over the land and ruthless, avaricious men turned the range into a blazing hell, and lives were cheap, with men dying with a surprising suddenness and—

Something moved at the very edge of his vision. At first, when he caught sight of it, he was not sure what it was. A vague shadowy form near the far side of the long barn. Then he saw a sudden splash of red-tongued flame, recognized one of the men there in the light of the torch he carried – Houston!

Grabbing his gunbelt, he swung it about his middle, buckled it quickly, threw on his jacket and ran from the room, shouting a warning at the top of his voice.

The door of the girl's room opened as he came level with it. Kathy stood framed in the opening. Her long hair was dishevelled and she had a robe wrapped tightly around her shapely body. Her eyes were wide with surprise. 'What is it, Frank?'

'Houston and some of his men,' he said harshly. 'They're out there now near the barn with torches. They're tryin' to fire the place. We've got to stop 'em.'

Running past her, he reached the outer door, jerked one of the pistols from its holster as he ran out on to the veranda. Crouching down, he began firing at the milling men in the distance. There was no doubting the other's intention now. Since the advantage of surprise had been lost by Slade's shout of warning and the fusillade of shots which he poured into them, there was no point in the outlaws keeping silent either and he could make out Houston's bull-like roar as he yelled orders to the men, waving his arms wildly as he urged them forward through the darkness.

Dust from the courtyard formed a silver screen around the men and it was impossible even to estimate accurately how many there were. For all he knew, there could be others moving in from another direction. He crouched down closer to the veranda rail, thumbed shells into the empty chambers of the hot gun. Near the bunkhouse on the other side of the courtyard, he saw a bunch of the Lazy Y men rush out into the open, scattering as they came under fire from Houston's men. McCorg was not visible with the men, but they came rushing towards the ranch, running in half crouch stance to present more difficult targets for the raiders.

Kneeling now, Slade gave them covering fire as they ran up to him, threw themselves down in the shadow of the house. Behind him, the girl had killed the lights inside the building itself and everything was in darkness, so that they were not outlined against lamplight, making silhouetted targets of themselves.

'You see who they are, Frank?' asked one of the men in a low voice.

'Sure. Houston is there with 'em. I suspect it's Weston and some of his crew.'

'But how in tarnation did they manage to get here so fast? They was still in town when we pulled out and I'll swear we weren't followed along the trail.'

'I guess there must be some other trail across the hills that we don't know about,' Slade said tersely. He aimed and fired at two men racing towards the bunkhouse, carrying flaming pitch torches. One of the men staggered as the slug found its mark, fell to his knees and rested there for a long moment, legs and arms twitching as he struggled to get back on to his feet. But his life and strength were ebbing from his body too quickly and he flopped forward and lay still, the brand burning fiercely on the ground in front of his prone body.

The barn had been set on fire. Three men, outlined by the flames, ran across the opening, tossed their burning brands inside, where they fell on the straw and set it afire.

Slade gritted his teeth in helpless anger as he saw the blaze flare up, knowing that it would be only a matter of minutes before the whole structure was ablaze and once the fire got a firm hold, as it undoubtedly would, there would be nothing they could possibly do to control it, even if they were able to get near it unhampered.

The quick, lean report of a Winchester sounded from somewhere close at hand and one of the trio gave up a great cry and rolled like a drunken man into the red-edged shadows near the barn. Slade glanced round swiftly, saw the barrel of the rifle thrust through one of the open windows. The girl's face was a pale grey blur in the darkness.

'Get back inside, Kathy,' he said harshly. 'Do you want to get your head blown off?'

Her reply was immediate. 'If you can risk your necks in an attempt to save the ranch from these killers, then I think I can. After all, this is my place now and I have a perfect right to defend it.'

There was no sense in trying to reason with her in her present mood, Slade knew that only too well. He swung on the men behind him, where they lay on the wooden boards of the veranda. 'We've got to get out there and try to drive 'em off, and then tackle that blaze. If we don't, the wind could whip those sparks in this direction and the ranch house will go. The wood here must be as dry as tinder.'

'That ain't goin' to be so easy,' growled one of the men, a black-bearded fellow. 'There must be close on a score of 'em and most are hiding in the shadows yonder where they have plenty of cover. They could shoot us down like sittin' ducks the minute we moved out.'

The firing burst up again with a sultry violence. Bullets hummed and whirred through the air just above Slade's head, cracked loudly against the walls of the house, chipped wooden splinters from the uprights of the porch. He saw the muzzle flashes of the guns in the distance on the far side of the courtyard. It was not going to be easy winkling those men out of there. He knew that firing the barn and bunkhouse was of secondary importance as far as the others were concerned. Their primary objective was to destroy everyone on the ranch, so that Houston could move in and take over without any more trouble.

Out in the corral, the horses were breaking under the frenzied rattle of gunfire. Slade could hear them pounding with their heels at the wooden fencing, knew it might not be long before they had it battered down and stampeded. If that happened, it would take them a long while to round them up once more, even if they drove off these men.

Thrusting his legs under him, he squirmed forward, reached the end of the veranda and hung there, poised for a long moment, aware of the spurting columns of dust less than two feet from his head where bullets pecked at the ground. Sucking in a deep breath, he held it in his lungs for a long moment and then kicked out and away from the porch, wriggling swiftly across the intervening open ground between himself and the water trough. He hit the ground hard, lay there for a moment while all of the enemy's fire seemed suddenly to be concentrated on him. Water splashed on to the back of his neck as several bullets struck the top of the trough.

The gunfire grew tremendous in its ear-splitting barbarity and the reek of stinking powdersmoke eddied across to Slade where he lay prone on the hard ground, pressing himself into the dirt, keeping his head as low as possible while death struck all about him. The crackling roar of the flames as they took a firm grip on the two buildings hammered at his ears and the light from the fires dispersed the shadows which normally lay over the courtyard.

In the glare of that light, it would be impossible to make a move without being seen at once. But there was no sense in waiting there any longer than necessary. Turning, he motioned to the men on the veranda behind him to give him covering fire. Then he drew himself up, dug in his heels once more, checked the sixgun and palmed it tightly. Gunshots blasted the night at his back and he saw two men, close to the door of the barn, stagger and crumple as bullets thudded into them. Then he was on his feet, running forward, the breath gushing hard and raw in his lungs and throat. Immediately, more gun blasts came from the direction of the barn and along the edge of the corral to his right. Bullets pecked at the dirt around his feet. Something scorched along his arm in a searing touch of pain. Then he had thrown himself bodily behind the pile of wood logs less than ten yards from the burning barn, twisting as he did so to get a good look at the tongues of flame that split the night. More men were visible in the distance, running forward, carrying brushwood torches. Behind them, he saw with a sense of shock, came six more, dragging a tall wagon of tinder-dry hay up to the top of the slope that overlooked the courtyard. Their intention was perfectly, blindingly, clear. They meant to fire the load of hay and then send the wagon rolling down towards the ranch house. Once it hit against the veranda, spilling its blazing contents out, there would be little chance of saving the house itself, and the men there, together with the girl, would have the choice of running out into the open where they could be cut down by well-aimed gunfire, or staying there and running the risk of being incinerated.

Seconds dragged by on slow, relentless feet. Lying on his chest, Slade remained cramped and tensed. He had to stop those men from carrying through their plan, but how? Already, two men were moving forward, holding themselves low, carrying the torches to fire the hay. He aimed swiftly, cut down one man, his limp body rolling down the slope, the sparks from the torch rising high into the air.

There was a low wire and post fence between the barn and the corral. A small bunch of Houston's men had squirmed into position there and were able to lay a blistering hail of fire across the courtyard.

Another shot came to slice a strip of wood from one of

the logs above his head as he crouched down, holding his breath, mind racing furiously. Lifting his head carefully, he peered between two of the tilted logs, saw the heads and shoulders of several men outlined above the wire fence as the men there jerked up to aim and fire, and then dropped back into cover.

'Hold your fire,' yelled a voice sharply. Slade stiffened as he recognized Houston's harsh tones. 'You out there, Slade?'

Behind the logs, Slade remained silent, tensed and taut. He had the idea that the other was feeling him out, wanting him to reply and then a fusillade of shots would pin him down while the rest of Houston's men rushed the ranch house.

'I know you're out there someplace, Slade. Listen to me. We've got this hay wagon here, ready to send it down into the ranch house. You can't stop us, so listen to my proposition. I want you to walk out here with your hands lifted high where I can see 'em. I want the girl, too, to come out. Once she's signed over the ranch and spread to me, she can go free. As for you, we've got a little score to settle and I'll see that you get a fair trial.'

You don't fool me for a single minute, Slade thought tightly. *As soon as I step out of cover, your men will cut me down and then you'll have a clear run.*

'I'm goin' to count up to ten, Slade. Then I'm sendin' in that wagon.'

Slade pulled his lips into a tight, hard line. Through a crack in the logs, he peered out into the lurid red glow that was spread over the courtyard, striving to see where the other was hidden. Maybe if he could kill Houston, the others would pull out. This was not their fight, they were only here to take orders, either from Houston, or more probably from Weston.

'One, two, three . . .' Houston began calling out in a low, monotonous tone.

Desperately, Slade tried to pin him down, but with the crackling of the flames in the vicinity, hearing was the most deceptive of the senses.

'Five, six, seven ... You don't have much longer to make up your mind, Slade.'

Slade moved further along the pile of logs. He could see the small group of men standing beside the loaded wagon. It was now poised on top of the rise, needed only a shove to send it rolling down the slope, gathering speed as it went. He switched his gaze from the wagon, looked back in the direction of the bunkhouse. Flames were licking around the doorposts but between them, resting his shoulder against one of the smouldering wooden uprights, he saw the tall figure of McCorg. The other had evidently been trapped inside the building when it had been fired, had probably been all but overcome by the smoke, but he was there now, his chest heaving as he dragged down the cooling night air into his lungs, and there was something in his right hand, something Slade could not see clearly, but which seemed to be glowing a little and giving off a train of sparks as he lifted his arm, swung his body back slightly and threw the object with all of his strength at the wagon.

A split second before Houston counted 'ten,' the stick of dynamite hit the ground near the waiting wagon, rolled beneath it, then detonated with a tremendous, ear-splitting explosion. Slade had dropped, an instant before the nation, throwing himself hard against the logs as the wagon was blown to pieces. Bits of debris fell around him. A long length of wood, splintered at either end, struck him on the shoulder. When he was able to lift his head and see again, there was little left of the wagon, or of the men who had been on the brow of the rise, standing around it. Further around the perimeter of the courtyard, Houston and Weston were yelling harshly to the rest of their men, shouting at them to stay where they were as the crew panicked and tried to run.

The tables had been turned on the outlaws now with a vengeance. McCorg had drawn his hand gun, was firing towards the men still crouched near the wire, taking them from the rear. Slade wanted to yell at the other to get down, to warn him that he was now outlined against the flames, presenting an excellent target but before the words would leave his lips, he saw McCorg stagger as Houston, whirling, shouted loud and fired from the hip.

Slade dived forward, hit the ground hard, rolled over, still clutching the heavy Colt, brought it to bear on the crooked marshal, loosed off a couple of shots, saw the other sway back out of sight. All along the side of the corral, the men were running, leaping across patches of shadow in their desperate hurry to get to their horses and ride out before they were killed.

Getting to his feet, Slade ran forward. His long legs carried him swiftly over the courtyard. Behind him, he heard the pounding feet of the rest of the Lazy Y crew as they ran to join him.

Houston fired at him and the flame of the muzzle blast lanced at him from the darkness. Then the other turned and ran, not wishing to make a hero of himself now that most of the men with him, had turned and deserted him. Out of the corner of his eye, Slide saw two men run from the direction of the corral. One yelled aloud as his jacket caught on the wire, holding him fast. He screamed in mortal terror, seeing death very close as the Lazy Y gunmen crowded close, firing as they came. With a super-human effort, he tore himself free of the clawing strands, lunged after his companion. Slade turned and as the man ran across the open door of the barn, presenting a good target, he fired instinctively. The man reeled back as if he had suddenly run into a brick wall, clutched at his chest and then sank bonelessly on to the ground, arms outstretched.

'Try to stop Houston and the others,' Slade yelled as the

rest of the men ran up to join him. 'I'm goin' to get McCorg.'

He raced past the side of the corral, ignoring the frantic stamping of the terrified horses there. He could just make out the inert form of the foreman inside the doorway, but he was still several yards away when a burning beam crashed down from the roof and collapsed between him and McCorg. Thrusting the Colt back into its holster, he leapt forward, jumped the blazing beam, went down on one knee beside the injured man. The smoke burned in his throat and lumps, got into his eyes, filling them with blurring tears so that it was almost impossible to see anything. Striving to hold his breath for as long as possible, he bent, got his hands under the other's shoulders and lifted him as gently as he could. It was impossible to see where the other had been hit, but as he moved him, he felt the sogginess of blood on the man's shirt front. The flames were so close now that they were searing his face and arms, the smoke choking him. He could feel his strength slipping from him like a rotten rag, his senses going. There was a roaring in his ears which was more than the sound of the flames as they ate avariciously at the bone-dry walls. The fire was spreading swiftly. Within minutes, the whole length of the bunkhouse would be an inferno and there would be no getting out.

Reaching down, trying not to think of what this would do to the other's chances of surviving if he had a bullet close to the heart or through the lungs, he heaved the other on to his toes, bent and took his inert weight across his shoulders, staggering under the burden.

Senses reeling, he staggered towards the smashed doorway. Flames formed a seemingly impassable barrier in front of him. He could not see anything beyond them, but something at the back of his mind, some insistent little voice that would not be stilled, told him that safety lay just beyond that wall of licking flame if only he could get through it, that on the other side the air was cool and sweet. For a moment, he almost fell, then he sucked in a deep breath of the superheated air, the sweat trickling down his forehead, running into his eyes in blinding streams, and lurched forward with McCorg's not inconsiderable weight balanced over his shoulders.

He felt the scorching finger of flame lick around his legs as he moved. His feet seemed to be on fire and it was as if he was walking forward over a bed of red-hot coals. He would never make it! It was too much to ask of any man to move through that terrible inferno. Unless he got out in a few moments, he would be unable to find the strength to get out himself, let alone with McCorg. Desperately, he lunged forward, feet slipping as he staggered from side to side. Flames seemed to be all over him, on his body and reaching up for his face. The whole world was one vast cauldron of fire.

He cannoned blindly into the side of the door, felt the post, almost burned through at the base, crack and shift under his careening weight. Then he was out and there was a welcome coolness on his face and body, hands caught at McCorg and took the other from him, and he collapsed on to the hard ground, unable to move a single muscle as other hands dragged him clear of the bunkhouse. Less than a minute later, the roof went in, sending up a billowing gush of flame and sparks high into the air. Fortunately, the bunkhouse lay to the north of the ranch house and the wind carried the sparks clear of the building. Sucking air down into his aching, tortured lungs, he forced his eyes open against the flickering red glare and looked about him, struggling desperately to retain a tight hold on his senses. There was the sound of shooting in the distance, the crashing reports clearly audible above the duller, more ominous sound of the fires which had been started. Weakly, he pushed himself to his feet. Kathy Curry came running over, caught him by the arm. There was a deep concern in

114

her voice as she gasped: 'Frank! Are you hurt?'

Shuddering a little, he shook his head. 'I've felt better, I must admit,' he said, forcing a wry grin. 'But I figure I'm all right. How's McCorg? He looked bad to me.'

'We'll get the doctor out from Cross Buttes to take a look at him,' Kathy said. 'He's badly hurt, but he's still alive, thanks to you.'

Two of the other men came back from the direction of the trail. They thrust their guns into leather, eyed Slade evenly. 'We killed twelve of the critters,' said Hank Silver, 'the others must've made it back to where they had their mounts tethered. No chance of overhaulin' any of 'em now before they hit town.'

Slade nodded. 'And what of Houston and Weston?'

Silver shrugged. 'Reckon they must've got clean away,' he said. There was a distinct note of disappointment in his voice.

'At least we beat them off and the ranch house is safe,' Kathy said in a low voice. She stood beside Slade and looked about her at the scene of devastation.

'They did enough damage,' Slade said tersely. A brief stab of pain along his arm reminded him that a bullet had earlier scorched the skin. There was a wide tear in the sleeve of his jacket and blood on his flesh.

Kathy saw it at once, noticed the dull sheen of blood there. Gripping his good arm a little more tightly, she led him back to the house. 'See that none of Weston's men are around, Hank,' she called over her shoulder.

Closing the door behind her, she went over to the sink and filled a basin with water, then took this over to the table and set it down close to the lamp she had just lit. Crooking her finger at Slade, she said: 'Sit down, Frank, and I'll clean that up for you.'

'It's nothin' more'n a scratch,' he said. 'Nothin' to make a fuss over. McCorg is badly hurt and you want to doctor me.'

'There's very little anyone here can do for McCorg until the doctor gets out here,' she said gravely, 'and that isn't likely to be before morning.'

Slade nodded. Crossing the room, he sat down and eased up the sleeve of his jacket. The injury was not serious, although the slug had bitten deep into the flesh, almost touching the bone. But it had bled copiously and Kathy washed it carefully. It still bled a little, but she soon proved herself to be quite expert with a bandage, working swiftly and speaking disinterestedly, almost casually as she said: 'What do you intend to do after tonight, Frank? Light back out to town and have it out with Houston?'

'I've been thinkin' along those lines,' he agreed.

'I thought perhaps you might.' She eyed him directly. 'Don't. He'll be waitin' for you to make such a move as that, hopin' you'll ride in and call him out. While he's in Cross Buttes, he's safe and he knows it. He has his friends around him there and you could be shot down from ambush long before you set eyes on him. He wants you for shooting down his brother.'

'Dan Houston asked for it,' Slade said calmly. But a little of the steel was beginning to show through his tone. 'What do you suggest that I ought to do? Sit tight here, hidin' behind a woman's skirts and waitin' for Houston to come to me? After tonight's work, he won't dare to show his face around here again. He sure won't get any men to follow him.'

'I hope you're right about that. We've lost a lot because of tonight. I suppose I ought to be thankful it wasn't more. The barn and the bunkhouse can be rebuilt. But if it had been the ranch house, that would have been a bitter blow.'

'You've got McCorg to thank for that. It was quick thinkin' to use that dynamite on the wagon. If he hadn't, it would have been the finish.'

The doctor came riding out from Cross Buttes shortly

before ten o'clock the next morning. He halted the buck-board in front of the house and climbed down, stiff-legged, standing for a long moment in the middle of the courtyard, looking about him at the burnt-out wrecks of the outbuildings. Then he shrugged as Kathy Curry came out on to the porch.

'You seem to have had a spot of trouble out here, Miss Curry,' he said conversationally. 'I heard a little talk in town before I left. Seems as though Houston was deter-mined to finish you that time.'

Kathy Curry smiled a little frostily. 'As you can see for yourself, he wasn't too successful. We can easily get more barns and a bunkhouse, but he lost a lot of men in the fighting and I doubt if he'll try anything like that again in a hurry.'

'Mebbe not,' agreed the other. He stepped up onto the porch beside her. 'Well, I reckon you'd better take me to my patient. I gather he's been shot pretty bad.'

Kathy Curry led the way into the bedroom at the side of the house, opened the door for him. Beside the bed, Slade glanced up as the doctor came in, gave the other a nod of greeting. 'Glad you got here, Doc,' he said. 'He's lost a lot of blood although we've done our best to try to staunch it.'

'All right, let me take a look at him,' fussed the other. He placed his bag on the small table beside the bed, then opened the other's shirt. In the light which filtered through the half open window, McCorg appeared to be already dead. Only when one looked closely at him was it possible to see the slight movement of his chest, rising and falling shallowly. He was deathly white, his eyes closed, his lips a strange blue shade.

The doctor nodded dryly. 'He's lost a lot of blood as you say,' he murmured, 'and it looks as if he's been shot through the lung. I'll have to dig for the bullet. Good thing he seems to be unconscious. But just in case he does happen to come round, think you can hold him down?

This isn't goin' to be easy.'

'I'll manage him, Doctor,' Slade said.

'Good. Now if you could get me some boilin' water, Miss Kathy.' He turned to the girl. She nodded and left the room.

As soon as she had gone, Slade said urgently: 'What do you reckon his chances are, Doctor?'

The other pursed his lips for a long moment, then said in a low voice which could not have been heard beyond the door. 'Very slender. I've known a lot of men recover from a bullet through the lungs. It's not out of the ordinary for them to heal naturally, if they get proper nursin' and don't try to get back into the saddle before I say they can. But he's lost blood, a lot of it.'

'Do what you can for him, anyway.'

'Of course.'

Kathy Curry came back with a bowl of steaming water and some clean cloths which she placed on the table beside the doctor's bag.

'Excellent,' murmured the other. Taking out a long, slender probe from his bag he dropped it into the boiling water, then took off his coat and rolled up his sleeves.

'You ready with him in case he comes round?' asked the other, stepping forward.

Slade nodded, stood behind McCorg, hands on the man's shoulders. He did not apply much pressure, merely stood ready to do so at any sign of movement from the injured man. It was a gruesome business, probing around for the bullet, embedded somewhere in the flesh. But fortunately, not until it was almost out, did the pain bite down through the curtain of unconsciousness and lance into the other's brain. He uttered a low moan deep in his throat and his eyes flicked open suddenly, staring up at them as they bent over him. Then he began to struggle, not weakly as Slade had expected from his physical condition, but with tremendous titanic heaves which made it difficult for him to hold the other down. Not until the doctor lifted the probe clear and dropped something on to the table with a metallic thud, was he able to relax.

'Not much to look at, is it?' said the other, stepping back. 'Such a little thing to have caused all of that trouble,' he paused, sighed as he rolled down his shirt sleeves. 'The thing is that so often it is the little things of the world that make the most trouble.'

Slade stared at him. 'And just what is that supposed to mean, Doc?' he asked.

The older man squinted upward at him, blinking a little against the lamp glow. 'I've tended and patched up more victims of gunfights than you can possibly realize in my lifetime,' he said slowly, 'and somehow I got the feelin' that few, if any, of those fights was really necessary. They'd all been caused by little things that had no real importance, but were enough for men to get themselves killed over. We're tryin' to build a decent country out west but there are always the lawless elements around who try to hold up progress. What they don't see is that you can't hold it up. It's comin' and all they are doin is delayin' it for a little while longer.'

'Trouble is that a man has to defend himself, or be shot down without a chance,' Slade said tautly.

The medical man nodded his head very slowly. His piercing blue gaze rested on Slade for a long moment and it was as if he were trying to make up his mind about him, as if something about the man who faced him, was puzzling him. At last, he nodded towards the bandage on Slade's arm. 'What happened to you?'

'Just a scratch. Kathy fixed it for me.'

'I see.' The other paused, then went on: 'You puzzle me, Slade. I've seen a great many different types of men come ridin' west into Cross Buttes. Some came to set up a new life here, movin' in with the wagon trains. Others came to get all they could out of the town and the territory and they weren't too particular how they did it or who they hurt in the process. I've seen lawmen and gunfighters move in, merchants and gamblers. But you don't fit into any of those categories and that's what puzzles me.'

'Maybe I'm not one of any of those types,' Slade said with a faint grin.

'Mebbe not,' agreed the other. 'You know how to handle a gun and you've got enough courage to stand up to crooked men like Weston and the Houstons to be some kind of a lawman. Yet I ain't seen you totin' any badge around, any authority to back up what you're doin'.'

Slade raised his brows a little. 'I wasn't aware that I was doin' anythin',' he observed. 'Except tryin' to avenge the death of my friend and help his daughter with the ranch.'

'You're doin' that passin' well,' the other conceded. He pulled out a curved pipe and began stuffing strands of tobacco down into the bowl with his forefinger, 'but I can't help feelin' that there's somethin' more to it than that. I think you're here to make trouble of some kind for Cross Buttes.'

'I'll do my best not to cause too much trouble,' Slade said softly. 'If there is to be any trouble, a lot is goin' to depend on what other people do.'

The doctor considered Slade's taut features, seemed to be turning over several replies to that statement in his mind, but when he spoke, it was only to say: 'I'll have a word with Miss Kathy before I leave. Good day, Mister Slade.'

After the doctor had returned to town, Slade went out into the corral, whistled up the bay and threw a saddle on it, tightening the cinch and checking the Winchester in its scabbard.

Kathy came out of the house and walked slowly towards him as he stood by the rail of the corral. 'Where are you going, Frank?' she asked, her voice small and tight.

'I've still got a chore to finish,' he said harshly. 'And I

120

figure that now is perhaps the best time to do it.'

'You're intending to ride into town and have it out with Houston and Cal Weston, aren't you?' There was something faintly accusing in her tone, and he stared at her in surprise. A moment later, she looked forlorn and helpless. 'Can't you see that I need you here, Frank. They'll kill you as soon as you ride into town, they may even have meen watching every inch of the trail to make sure you don't get as far as Cross Buttes. Houston wants you dead and he doesn't much care how it's done. And if he succeeds, what can I do then? With my foreman lying in there with a bullet hole in his body.'

'Kathy.' He took her arms and made her face him, then tilted her face up as he put a hand under her chin. 'There are some things that a man has to do and very often he isn't in a position to explain them at the time. Then people just have to trust him. Can you understand that?'

Her lower lip trembled a little. 'I think so. But be careful. Houston is a cunning devil. He'll stop at nothing to kill you.'

He studied the statement and tried to answer it, and could not. He held his silence for a matter of minutes and at last, swinging himself up into the saddle, he said: 'I think I know how to handle Chuck Houston. He's the type of man who gets others to do his dirty work for him. He won't come out and face me like a man. He'll be like his brother, skulking in the shadows, ready to jump out and pump a couple of slugs into my back when he figures I'm lookin' the other way. I've met that kind before on many occasions.'

'That's why he can be so dangerous,' she said. 'Cal Weston must still be in town and he'll be smartin' from the beating he and his men took last night. It must have reduced his crew strength by half and he's vulnerable now. If I was to give the word, we could sweep down and take him without too much trouble.'

'But you won't do that,' he said quietly, resting his gaze on her.

'Why not?' she retorted strongly. 'He killed my father. He was the man who pulled the rope. You can talk to me about Houston sitting at the centre of the web pulling all of the strings and giving the orders, but Weston was the man we considered our friend, who turned on us and tried to destroy us completely. I want him dead, more than I want to see Chuck Houston die.'

Looking down at her, with the strong sunlight touching her face with light and shadow, he felt the strength of her will, tough and inflexible, and for the first time, he felt a little afraid that she might do something rash, just to ensure that Cal Weston paid the full price for what he had done. Then he nodded slowly, touched spurs to his mount and rode out of the courtyard.

SIX

TREACHERY

Frank Slade pushed his mount along the dried-up bed of a creek, giving his mount its head as it picked its way over the smooth, treacherous stones that glistened whitely in the scorching sun. Every now and again, he turned in the saddle and peered into the shimmering heat haze at his back, looking for any sign of pursuit, knowing that it was possible for Houston to have spent the last part of the night in the brush close to the Lazy Y, watching the trail, ready to pounce as soon as anyone rode out. But there was no sign of any pursuers. That meant little, as he could not see very far in that direction, but at least he saw no dust and this meant that if anyone was there, they were not coming up very fast on him and he would have plenty of warning.

At noon, he rested up beside a narrow, swift-flowing creek that ran across his trail, letting the horse graze on the lush green grass that grew near the bank. He did not build a fire, being too close to the trail, and ate cold, jerked beef, washed down with water from the stream.

He smoked a cigarette, then got to his feet, climbed back into the saddle and rode deep into the pines, travelling without haste, thinking things out in his mind, trying to assess every probability, so that he would not make any mistake once he reached town. The girl's words came back to him, and he recognized the truth in them. Houston was the cunning, cold-thinking type who would prefer other men to carry out his killings for him. If that were so, then it might prove very difficult to get through to him.

The red-bodied pines lay thickly now on all sides of him, crowding in on the trail, branches shouldering down at him, so that in places he was forced to ride with his head low, crouched over the neck of his mount. There was a deep and clinging silence all about him, except for the sharp hammer of a woodpecker somewhere in that deep aromatic greenness beneath the overhead canopy of leaves that shut out most of the sunlight, allowing only a little to filter through.

An hour later, he came out on the edge of a long, low ridge. The main desert trail lay below him, a grey scar in the strong sunlight. He paused, reining up, and let his glance range over it. Then he narrowed his eyes, got down and walked right up to the very edge. Almost directly below him, he spotted the low-roofed, broken-down shack, evidently one of the many broken-down, forgotten cabins which had been thrown up by some prospector. There was a square area of cleared ground, surrounded by stakes, many of which were now sharply angled, where they had fallen. A couple of trees stood close by, on one side of the shack, and in one of them, the head rusted by wind and rain, an axe was embedded. There was no way of telling what had happened to the man who had thrown up this log-and-shake cabin, but it was no longer deserted. There were six horses tethered to the slanted rail outside and the marks of men in the dust that lay about the building.

He crouched down, watching the scene below through his lawman-trained eyes. He felt certain that those horses belonged to men from Weston's spread even though he could not see their brand marks. There was no sign of the owners of the horses and he guessed they were inside. For a moment, he crouched there, deliberating, then took the horse further back into the trees, tethered it securely to one of the saplings, then catfooted back to the ledge. For several moments, he scouted around, then spotted the narrow, dangerous track which led down from the top of the ridge towards the shack. For a while, Slade crouched there considering this, then decided to take his chance. It might be the only chance he would get of trapping these men, catching them together. Very carefully, he let himself down the steep slope, making little noise, not wanting to alert any of the men inside the shack. It was very quiet. The muscles under his chest drew tight. If any of those men were to step outside, they were sure to see him; in the glaring sunlight, it would be impossible for them not to spot him.

Inside the shack, there was utter silence. Although he paused once, clinging tenaciously to out-thrusting roots to steady himself, straining his ears, he could pick out no sound. The silence was instantly noticeable. To any man trained and raised on the frontier, reared in an atmosphere of tension, it was second nature to attune oneself to the changing moods of the countryside. There were no birds flying to indicate that they had been disturbed during the past few minutes and this was something which Slade noticed more than anything else.

Five minutes later, he reached the level ground at the base of the ridge, crouched down for a moment to regain his breath, then moved forward, eyes and ears alert. He tested the shadows which lay all about the shack and also took note of the tumble-down shed which had been built close to the wall of rock at the rear of the cabin. Danger was out here. He could feel it all about him.

Drawing his sixgun, he moved around the side of the cabin, approached the shed at the back. It had obviously been built to house a horse and a burro. There were piles of rotting hay lying around the floor and the smell of rottenness and decay was strong in his nostrils when he moved inside. A quick look around convinced him that it was empty and the dust across the entrance had not been disturbed. He made a leisurely examination of the shed, looked for another way out in case he was surprised, but found none. Backed up against a wall of solid rock, there was not enough space for a cat to squeeze through let alone a man, and it had been surprisingly well built for such a small, inconsequential structure.

Passing across to the opening again, he glanced out, eyes narrowed against the flooding sun glare. Going down on one knee, he strained to pick up the sound of men moving around inside the shack, now less than ten feet away. At first, he could hear nothing beyond the soft noises of the horses tethered to the rail at the front of the cabin. Then he picked out the faint murmur of conversation and nodded to himself in satisfaction.

Straightening up, he soft footed forward, palming his sixgun tightly in his right fist. Reaching the door of the shack, he saw that it was partly ajar and stood for a moment with his shoulder pressed close to the wooden wall. He heard Houston's unmistakable bull-like voice say: 'He's sure to come ridin' along this stretch of trail, Weston, if he means to head back into town.'

'But what makes you all-fired sure that he'll ride into town? He'll be a goddamned fool if he does. He must know we'll be waitin' for him there, that he won't stand a chance in hell of gettin' out alive.'

'I know how this *hombre* thinks,' grated the other. There was the sound of a rickety wooden chair creaking as somebody shifted their weight around in it. 'I say we only have to wait another hour or so and he'll be along; and when he does come, we'll be ready for him.'

'I hope you're right, Houston. If you're not, then we'll have wasted time.' There was a trace of bitterness audible in the other's tone. 'You seem to forget that I lost nearly half of my force last night, followin' you in that attack on the Lazy Y spread. I should have thought twice about it before agreein' to your idea.'

'Don't talk like a danged fool, man,' muttered Houston. 'It was sheer bad luck that somebody spotted us before we were ready to move in. If it hadn't been for that, we'd have had 'em cold. That place would've been burnt out by now and Slade would be finished. As it is—'

'As it is, he's right here.' Slade kicked open the door and stepped into the dim interior of the shack, letting his glance roam quickly around the men at the table. 'Now don't anybody make any sudden moves towards their guns. If they do, I might just be sufficiently itchy-fingered as to pull this trigger. Just back away slowly and keep your hands in sight.'

The men did as they were told. One glance at the face of the man who stood in the doorway was enough to tell them with a sudden certainty that any false move on their part would be their last.

Darkly, Houston said: 'You're makin' a big mistake comin' in here like this, Slade. I've already got a warrant here for your arrest on a charge of murder. Actin' like this ain't goin' to help your case any.'

'You can keep your warrant, *Marshal*,' said Slade; 'when I'm through it won't be of any use to you.' His voice, as he spoke, was coldly brittle.

'You don't scare me at all, Slade,' gritted the other. He held his hands wide from his body, but his narrowed eyes flicked from one man to another in the room. 'There are more of us than you can deal with. Even if you drop one of us, the others' will get you. Or have you considered that?'

'I've considered it, Houston,' Slade nodded. 'I know your kind. You're tryin' to get some of your men to rush me, hopin' to get your gun while I'm shootin' them down. I wouldn't advise you to hope too much. The first wrong move any of these men makes, and you get it beween the eyes.' He cocked the gun in his hand as he spoke, the click of the hammer making an unnaturally loud sound in the room. A faint expression of fear crossed the other's broad, fleshy features. He went on quickly: 'How long do you figure you can hold us here, Slade? When we're missed in town, there'll be another posse out lookin' for us. We know that you rode out of the Lazy Y ranch alone. Nobody will bother to come lookin' for you if you don't get back there before nightfall.'

'You talk too much, Houston,' Slade said. He switched his gaze suddenly to Weston. The big rancher was eyeing him sullenly from the corner of the room. 'As for you, Weston, I reckon that Miss Curry would willingly pull the trigger that sends you into eternity and not think twice about it. Maybe that would be real justice. Turn you over to her and the men from the Lazy Y. I hear they had a great deal of affection for Ed Curry. I'm sure they'd all know how to deal with his murderer.'

'You're bluffin', Slade,' said the other harshly. He swallowed nervously and his glance fell to the gun in Slade's hand. 'You got no proof of what happened in Cross Buttes when Ed Curry was hung.'

'No? I'm sure that when Houston here is finished, there'll be plenty of good, solid citizens in town who will be only too willin' to talk and tell all they know. Once they realize that your reign of terror is finished, they'll want to be rid of the lot of you.'

Weston's features twisted into a sudden grimace of indecision. He spun on Houston. 'Nobody is goin' to hang me for what you ordered, Houston,' he said thickly, through trembling lips. 'You got half of my men killed because of your wild ideas and then—'

'Shut up, you goddamned fool!' snapped the marshal. 'Can't you see that this is just what he wants us to do, quarrel among ourselves and pass the blame. It gives him the proof he needs. If we stick together and say nothin', there ain't a thing he can do.'

'Don't be too sure of that, Houston,' said Slade sharply. 'Do you reckon that you can go on indefinitely, hidin' out here without anybody findin' out who you really are?'

'What do you mean by that?' For a moment, the other's well-maintained front of complete confidence in himself, cracked. His face bore the look of a hunted animal. Then the mask slipped back again.

'I mean that you're wanted for murder and robbery in almost half a dozen states. I was sent out here to clean up this place. I don't wear a badge, but I still have my credentials from the State Governor and they will overrule any warrant you may have trumped up for my arrest.' He gestured with the barrel of the gun towards the gunbelts which the other men wore. 'And while we're about it, I guess you'd better shuck those gunbelts in case anybody has any ideas of becomin' a dead hero.'

He watched closely as the men unfastened their gunbelts. Houston's was the first to fall, clattering on to the floor at his feet. The other men followed suit.

'Now what do you intend to do with us?' asked Houston, still assuming an air of complete confidence.

'I could shoot you down where you stand, Houston,' he said tersely. 'I got no quarrel with any of these men except for Weston and yourself.'

Houston shook his head slowly, deliberately. 'You're not the type to shoot down a man in cold blood, Slade. You live by the code of the gun, always give your opponent an equal chance. It makes you feel better that way and absolves you from any feelin' of guilt after you've committed murder.'

'I wouldn't bank on that. Such treatment isn't for men like you and Weston, men who pretend to be a man's friend and then lynch him.' The tight anger in his voice brought the uncertainty back to Houston's face. 'But I figure that the townsfolk in Cross Buttes should know what kind of men you are and I reckon they'll mete out justice to such low-down coyotes.'

'You'll never get away with this, Slade,' said Weston.

'I think I will.' Slade backed towards the door. 'I'm lockin' you all in that shed at the back. I've taken a good look at it, and I figure it will hold you without any trouble. And I assure you there's no other way out of it, unless you care to start tryin' to drill your way through solid rock.'

He faced them down, then motioned towards the door with the gun. Houston glared murderously at him for a long moment. He seemed on the point of hurling himself at his captor, gun or no gun, then held himself in with a tremendous effort. He moved behind the others, muttering hoarsely to himself as he stepped out into the glaring sunlight.

Herding the men into the shed, Slade dropped the iron pins into their staples, then turned and walked back to the shack. Even if those men did eventually manage to work themselves free he would make sure they did not reach town until long after nightfall by spooking their horses. Reaching the front of the shack, he patted the neck of the nearest horse, untied the rope which held it to the rail. It was then that he caught the sudden movement at the corner of his vision, the sharp flash of sunlight on the metal of a drawn gun. Not until that moment, did it come to him that there had been only five men in the shack, while outside, there had been tethered six horses.

Cursing himself for his carelessness and forgetfulness, he dropped at once, went for his gun. The hidden man had obviously seen what was happening and had waited his chance for Slade to come into his sights. The other's gun exploded in the same moment that Slade dropped and he felt the wind of the bullet's passing as he hit the ground, rolled over and loosed off a couple of quickly-aimed shots at the other. The sudden sound sent the horse near him jerking hard on the rope that held it to the rail and, shocked and scared, it reared high on its hind legs, pawing at the air.

Desperately, seeing his danger, he tried to wriggle away from the frenzied creature. But before he could do so, the animal began to gyrate savagely, lashing with its feet. Slade hurtled himself backward, but one of the slashing hoofs took him on the side of the head, caught him a glancing blow, not hard enough to crush the skull, but sufficiently hard to send him sprawling on the ground as he struggled vainly to keep his senses from becoming submerged in a deep and boundless sea of utter blackness.

When consciousness returned, there was a savage throbbing in his head which brought a wave of nausea surging from the pit of his stomach up into his chest. He gagged on it for a moment, tasted the bitter taste in his mouth. His senses cleared slowly. He was lying on his back on something hard and when he opened his eyes, he could make out nothing definite for a long moment. Then he was able to focus his gaze on a pair of riding boots that stood close to his face and, looking higher, he saw the sneering face of Chuck Houston grinning down at him from what seemed an incredible height. There was a gun in the other's hand and it was lowered so that the round black hole looked ominously close and large, trained on his head.

'You made a damned good try, Slade. But you forgot that nobody would shack up in a place like this to talk tactics without havin' one man at least out there watchin' the trail. You're dumber than I figured.'

He laughed harshly. Turning to someone Slade could not see, he said quietly: 'I reckon you'll find his horse somewhere up on top of the ridge, back among the trees a piece. He wouldn't be so stupid as to leave it loose where it could be spotted from down here. That's right, ain't it, Slade?'

When he said nothing in reply to the question, Houston drew back his foot and kicked the man at his feet in the small of the back, just above the kidneys. A savage spasm of agony shot through the lower half of Slade's body and then lanced up into his back and chest, biting through him. The sweat started out on his forehead and it was all he could do to bite down on the cry of pain that rose unbidden to his lips.

'Reckon that you'd better answer if you know what's good for you, Slade,' said the other ominously. 'Is that where your horse is?'

'Yes, damn you.' His voice sounded thin and weak. He tried to roll over on to his side to ease the pain in his body, then struggled up to a sitting position, expecting a further kick from the other, but Houston seemed content to let him sit up with his back against the wall.

The man Houston had earlier addressed went out and a moment later, Slade heard the unmistakable sounds of him climbing the steep slope at the rear of the shack. With an effort, he forced himself to think clearly. The man who had taken him by surprise outside, now lounged in the doorway. A man of medium height, slim build, with a hard, sharp-planed face and eyes set close together against the bridge of a long nose.

'Can I stand up now?' Slade asked tautly.

Houston considered that for a moment, then nodded, stepping back a little. 'I guess so, Slade, if you can make it.' He grinned viciously, kept the barrel of the gun lined up on the other, not taking any chances. 'Once we get your horse we'll ride on into town. I guess I can promise you as short a trial as Curry got. Then we'll take care of the girl.'

'You'll never get away with it.' Slade got to his feet, clinging to the wall for support as pain lanced through him at the movement.

Houston's grin widened. 'That's what you said yourself a few minutes ago, Slade. You saw for yourself how things can change very quickly.'

Presently, there was a sound outside the shack. The man at the door turned, said: 'Here's Al with the horse, Marshal.'

'Good. Let's get out of here. The sooner I have this *hombre* in jail, the better I'll like it.'

'Why?' said Slade hoarsely. 'Afraid that the Lazy Y crew will catch up with you sooner than you figure?'

He saw the other's bunched fist coming in a short, hard swing, but lacked the strength to avoid it. Knuckles grazed his cheek and the force of the blow flung him hard against the wall. The whole side of his face felt as though it was on fire as he picked himself up, glaring murderously at the other. Half a dozen guns swung and covered him, preventing him from hurling himself at the other.

'Now get outside, Slade, and don't make any funny moves or they'll be your last,' Houston warned, breathing heavily.

Leaning forward the Town Marshal jabbed Slade hard in the midriff with the barrel of his gun, forced him to the door. Outside, Slade's horse was waiting.

'Get mounted up,' ordered Houston. He jerked a thumb towards Weston. 'Cal here is goin' to rope your hands, just in case you should take it into your head to try to make a break for it before we get to town.'

Slade twisted his lips a little as Weston used a piece of thin, strong cord to bind his wrists in front of him. He knew from the way the other tied them that those knots would never be undone, no matter how hard he worked on them along the trail into town. Houston's plan was only too obvious. Once he got him inside that jail, another lynching party would be formed and he would go the same way as Ed Curry. There was no way the girl could help him now. She had warned him against this venture but he had ridden into trouble with his eyes shut in spite of her warnings. Now he had only himself to blame.

A few minutes later, they rode out of the small clearing, hit the main trail a quarter of a mile further on, and rode towards Cross Buttes at a fast gallop. They rode in silence, each man engrossed in his own thoughts. In spite of the futility of his actions, Slade continued to tug at the cord around his wrists, striving to stretch it sufficiently to allow him to slip his hands out of it, but it had been tied too tightly for him to make any impression on it whatsoever and after a while he was forced to give up, his wrists chafed and bleeding.

Presently, he said loudly: 'Just what is it you figure to get out of this, Houston? You intendin' to take over the entire territory?'

'Sure.' The other uttered a harsh laugh, half turned in his saddle. 'And why not? There's nobody here can stop me now. I had you figured for a dangerous man when you first rode into town, but it seems I was mistaken. You're just like all of the others, too easy to take.'

'I wouldn't be too sure of that, Houston.' Slade's tone had a steely ring to it and for a brief moment, the marshal stared directly at him, eyes searching his face, trying to find some hidden meaning behind the other's words. Then he twisted his lips into a grin.

'You don't frighten me none, Slade. Not now. I'm the law in town and I guess I can always turn the other way if some of the boys decide they want to take things into their own hands. You got to understand that a few of 'em are a little quick when it comes to handin' out justice.'

'I gathered that when I heard what happened to Ed Curry,' Slade said evenly. He kept his eyes on Weston as he spoke, saw the red flush spread up from the rancher's neck, suffusing his broad, fleshy face.

Turning sharply in his saddle, his hand hovering close to the gun at his waist, Weston said thinly: 'Just give me the chance here and now, Houston. This *hombre* is talkin' too much.'

134

'Don't let him rile you, Cal. Maybe he wants it quick and sudden. But the way we got it figured for him in town will be slow enough for him to have to think about it, knowing it's comin' to him, but not knowin' how and when. We can afford to let him stew a while.'

'Can we?' retorted the other. 'What happens if he did leave word with the Lazy Y to ride into town if he didn't get back before a certain time? Still reckon we could hold off that bunch if they came a-ridin'?'

'They won't,' Houston replied confidently. 'He's only tryin' to rattle us.'

There was silence after that. Inwardly, Slade had hoped that he might have sown a seed of doubt in the minds of the men riding with Houston and Weston, knowing that these men had no axe to grind as far as he, personally, was concerned. But it seemed clear that he had failed. With him in their hands, any danger to their position seemed to have abruptly evaporated.

Three hours later, they rode into the main street of Cross Buttes. A few loafers along the boardwalks stared in curious interest at the group of riders, watching the man who rode with his hands tied in front of him, staring straight ahead of him. In front of the sheriff's office, Houston reined up his mount, slid from the saddle, moved up on to the boardwalk, then turned and motioned Slade to dismount. The rest of the men, with the exception of Cal Weston, remained seated, eyes on Slade as he dropped heavily to the ground. His head was still throbbing painfully from the glancing kick he had received from the terrified horse and pain lanced through his body with every step he took.

'When do I get my hands untied?' he asked shortly, standing in the dusty street, looking up at the marshal.

'Just as soon as I get you inside that cell,' replied the other. He turned and unlocked the door of the office, pushing open the door and stepping inside. Cal Weston came up behind Slade, thrust the barrel of his gun into the other's back and shoved him inside, closing the door behind him.

Picking up the bunch of keys from behind his desk, Houston led the way to the cells at the rear of the building, opened one of the doors, stood on one side as Slade was jabbed forward. Not until the other was in the cell did he take the long-bladed knife from his belt and slash through the ropes that bound Slade's wrists. Then the door clanged shut on him; a sound that was a knell to Frank Slade's ears.

'You meanin' to keep me here without anythin' to eat and drink?' he asked, staring through the bars at the two men standing in the passage.

Houston rubbed a hand over his chin, then shrugged. 'Now that you're here I guess we can give you somethin'. Don't want a starvin' man on my hands.'

Once he had eaten, Slade leaned back on the low bunk in the cell, fit a cigarette and tried to think things out in his mind. There was no disguising the precariousness of his position. There could be no possible help from Kathy Curry and her crew. It would be another day at least, possibly longer, before they might decide to ride into town and see for themselves what had happened, and he felt certain in his mind that he would be hanging from the end of a riata long before then. Houston would take no chances with him; yet he would have to make it look good before the townsfolk. Two lynchings in the space of a month or so would look extremely bad for Houston, as Town Marshal, especially when the circuit judge arrived. It would not be easy to explain the lax way in which the other guarded his prisoners, allowing two of them to be taken out and hanged without a proper trial.

The late afternoon sun threw a slanting pattern of light through the barred window over his head and as he lay there, the smoke curling up to the ceiling from his cigarette, he watched the patch of light on the far wall move with an inexorable slowness as the sun sank. Soon it would be dark and he had the feeling that this would be when Weston and his cronies would make their attempt. Already, he could feel that noose beginning to tighten around his neck.

Bitterly he could only reflect on the foolishness, the carelessness, of his rash actions in trying to tackle all of those men at once in the miner's shack. His one hope had been to ride into town and convince the people there of Weston's guilt and Houston's implication in the murder of Ed Curry. There must be many townsfolk who had liked Curry. Even though he had been a big man as far as ranchers went, he had been fair and well-liked in the days when Slade had known him. Not until Houston had arrived with his brother had things changed in Cross Buttes.

Now he was in a horrible mess with no possible way out. There was an inevitability about everything that was frightening. Every move he had made had been apparently countered by Houston. He wondered if word of his capture and arrest had reached the doctor. At least, he was a man who might have the guts and the inclination to ride out to the Lazy Y and warn Kathy of what had happened. But it was a very slim chance and he knew better than to bank on it.

The sunlight, streaming through the window, became redder and fainter as the sun sank over the Elklands. It would be completely dark within the hour. There was the sound of someone knocking loudly on the street door. He heard the commotion, then the scrape of a chair in the outer office as Houston got to his feet to answer it. There was the murmur of conversation, Houston's voice raised a little and another voice, which Slade did not recognize through the closed door at the end of the passage, answering him.

137

A few moments later, the other man evidently had his way, for the passage door opened and there was the sound of booted feet in the corridor. Tensed a little, Slade got to his feet. Moving forward, he gripped the bars of the cell tightly, peering out into the gloom of the corridor in an attempt to see who was with Houston. He heard the marshal grumbling a little under his breath, but there was also the unmistakable clank of the keys he was carrying and the tension in Slade's mind increased.

Houston fumbled with the keys in the lock, then swung the door open, stepping to one side.

'Seems the Doc wants to have a look at you, Slade,' he said harshly. 'I wouldn't have allowed it, but we don't want a man goin` to the rope without having his wounds tended to, do we?' He laughed hoarsely. 'Better make a good job of him, Doc. I want him to know exactly what's happenin' to him when that rope tightens around his neck. He killed my brother and this time, I'm goin' to be right there, watchin' when—'

The other broke off sharply, gave a low, bleating cough and fell forward as the reversed Colt in the doctor's hand descended on the back of his skull. Reaching down, Slade grabbed him swiftly, hauled his unconscious body into the cell, then stepped out into the corridor, slamming the door behind him. turning the key in the lock.

'Thanks, Doc,' he said quietly. 'I don't know why you did that, but—'

'There's no time now for lengthy explanations, Slade. Let's say that I was a friend of Ed Curry's. Now you must get away, out of town. Weston and his men are over at the saloon. but they could come along any minute. You'll find your guns on the desk in the office. Now hurry.'

All the time he had been speaking, the other had been pushing Slade along the passage and into the outer office.

Buckling on his gunbelt, Slade checked the weapons, balanced them for a moment in his hands, then stepped towards the street door, moving carefully.

'You sure about Weston's men, Doc?' he asked tautly.

'Yes.' The other drew his brows slightly downward. 'I saw them bring you into town but I had to wait until the rest of the men were safely out of the way before I could do anything.'

'I'd say you made your move just in time,' Slade said softly. 'Unless I'm mistaken, Weston is already tryin' to whip up another lynchin' party in the saloon yonder. Houston was to stay in the office and be ready when they arrived.'

'The same pattern as with Ed Curry,' nodded the other. He thrust his head a little way out of the door, stared up and down the quiet street. 'The ways of violence, Mister Slade. They never change, yet them seem to be always changing. I wonder at times if there is ever going to be any hope for towns like this, if we will become civilized.'

'It will come,' Slade said confidently. 'But first we have to get rid of men such as Houston and Weston as we would wild animals who no longer have any right to live.'

'I can't say that I agree with killing them like that, but when I see how justice has become perverted here, then I know I'm not in any position to say anything against that course of action. Now you'd better hurry before somebody comes. Once those men in there are sufficiently whipped up for a lynchin' they'll be across here lookin' for Houston.'

Nodding, Slade began to move slowly along the front of the building. The street was, for the most of its length, completely empty. A few yellow lights were beginning to show in the windows on either side of it, cutting swathes of radiance through the growing gloom. His mount had been taken from in front of the sheriff's office and he knew that if he was to get out of town, he would have to take another. One more crime to add to the list which Houston had pinned on him, that of horse-thieving.

Turning his head, he caught a glimpse of the doctor making his way quickly to the other side of the street, vanishing into the shadowy opening between two of the buildings. Clearly the other did not wish to be implicated as yet in his escape. Once Houston came round and found himself locked in his own cell, he would give the alarm and then the doctor would be implicated. By that time, it was up to Slade to do something about it. He figured that three hours' hard riding would take him back to the Lazy Y. Then it would be the time for the big showdown.

Reaching the end of the block, he paused for a moment, peering off into the dark shadowy alley to his left. Nothing moved there, no man-silhouette. He darted across the gaping alley mouth, reached the boardwalk on the far side and cat-footed along it, keeping his head low, his body in a half crouch. Now that he had his guns buckled about him, he felt better. At least. he could always make a fight of it, probably take Weston with him.

About a hundred yards along the street, he saw the shadowy shapes of a bunch of horses hitched to the rail outside one of the stores. If he could reach them, there was a good chance. Spooking the others would delay any pursuit.

Halfway there. he paused as a sudden commotion behind him caused him to flatten himself to the wall of the store. The doors of the saloon on the other side of the street opened and a flood of men poured out. Weston was there, he could see the tall shape of the rancher, haranguing the men, gesturing with his arms as he pointed towards the jail. It was impossible for Slade to pick out the other's words, but he could guess at what the rancher was telling the men.

Slade went on, straight into the darkness for another fifty feet, came upon the horses suddenly. He was reaching for one, when a shadow detached itself from the gloom. He had no warning of any kind, had not expected anyone to be there guarding the horses. For a moment, he stood still, trying to recognize the man. The other came forward, spotted him, said in a low tone: 'Weston ready for me to move up with the horses?'

'Sure.' Slade said softly. 'I've to help you with the critters.' He moved down into the street, so as to come alongside the other. The man was still not suspicious, merely jerked a thumb in the direction of the further group of horses. 'You take that bunch along,' he said. 'I'll manage these all right.'

'All right,' said Slade. He drew level with the other, waited until the man had turned his back on him to untie the hitching rope, then withdrew his Colt, striking the other hard on the side of the head. The man's knees collapsed under him and he fell forward against the flank of the horse without a murmur. Stepping to one side, Slade caught him before he fell, lowered the other's inert body to the ground and patted the horse on the neck as it shied away instinctively.

'There, there, boy,' he said in a quiet, soothing tone. 'It's all right.'

The horse calmed at his words, stood shivering a little, but made no further movement or sound. Untying the ropes, Slade stepped back. He drew in several deep breaths, stared back along the street. The crowd of men were still there in the middle of the roadway.

He swung himself up into the saddle, leaned forward to pull the others away from the hitching rail and at that moment, Weston's voice from along the street, reached him.

'Get those horses along, Al.'

Slade saw the other clearly silhouetted against the light from the saloon. Then he hauled on the rope, slapped the nearest horse sharply on the flank. It lunged away and a few seconds later, the rest followed, thundering in a rising cloud of dust along the street and out of town.

'It's Slade!' Weston yelled. 'Shoot him down, men! Somebody go across to the jail and see what's happened to the marshal.'

Slade saw the men in the roadway scatter at the other's sharp-voiced command. Several shots whistled along the street towards him as they commenced firing and he heard the vicious, wicked hum of slugs tearing through the air close to his head as he fought to control his bucking mount. Men began running towards him, firing from the hip as they came. He aimed his own gun at their muzzle flashes, saw two of them stagger and crumple as they fell, gunshot, all the life gone from them before they hit the ground.

Out of the corner of his eye, Slade spotted Weston, running forward a little way, then dodging in towards the shadows of the boardwalk. Lead screeched about Slade as he drew his lips back over his teeth. Weston fired only once. Then with a harsh, bleating cry, he dropped his gun from nerveless fingers, turned in a half circle and staggered drunkenly across the street, arms stretched blindly in front of him, moving through the curtain of gunfire as if it did not exist. He had taken perhaps half a dozen unsteady paces when he collapsed suddenly on his face and lay still.

SEVEN

GUNFIGHT AT CROSS BUTTES

Swinging his mount's head, Slade kicked at its flanks with his spurs, sending it lunging forward into the darkness. A roll of shots sounded at his back as the men continued to fire, but moments later, he was out of town, riding up into the towering rocks that lifted along the trail. He rode swiftly, sorry for his mount, but knowing that he had very little time. Events had moved more swiftly than he had anticipated and a lot was going to depend on the next few hours. Once that mob in town released Houston, the marshal was going to do all he could to collect as large a force as possible to ride out to the Lazy Y and fulfil his earlier attempt at destroying it.

There was a moon now, giving him enough light to see by. The trail was, in places, little more than a faintly seen grey scar across the rocky desert. But he drove his mount headlong towards the north, spurring it on whenever it showed sign of flagging. Only once did he rein up, on a high, rocky outspur that looked down on to the flatness of the rolling desert at his back. But even in the flooding moonlight, he could see nothing there beyond his own dust trail. He sat there for several seconds like a man exhausted beyond his ability to move; then raked rowels across his horse's flanks, and rode down the slope. This was the way of it for almost three hours, before he finally rode into the courtyard of the Lazy Y. There was still the unmistakable smell of smoke hanging in the air and the burnt-out hulk of the barn loomed on his right as he slid from the saddle on the run.

He was still several yards from the ranch, when the door opened. Kathy Curry stood framed in the light that spilled out. Then, as though realising that if this were an enemy she presented an excellent target, she stepped instantly to one side on to the porch.

'Frank?' she called loudly. 'Is that you?'

'It's me, Kathy,' he said, striding quickly forward. He went up on to the porch beside her, his boots echoing hollowly on the wooden slats.

'What happened? You look as though you've been riding hard.'

'Weston's dead,' he said quietly. 'They were holed up in a miner's shack a few miles from here. I managed to surprise 'em, but they had one man holed up outside to watch the trail. He took me unawares and they dragged me off to the jail in town, no doubt to suffer the same kind of fate as your father.'

'Then how in heaven did you get away?' she asked incredulously.

'The doctor. He talked Houston into lettin' him come to the cell to tend a bump on my head, then knocked Houston cold with his gun. I spooked their horses, but it won't be long before they round up more.'

'And when they do?'

'My guess is that they'll come ridin' out here to finish the job they started last night.'

'And what do you mean to do? We have the rest of the men, but will they be enough to hold off the men that Houston will bring with him?'

'I doubt it. He can form a posse now, swear in some of the townsfolk. I broke out of jail and stole a horse. That's enough evidence for him to make a criminal out of me in the eyes of the citizens of Cross Buttes.' There was a trace of bitterness in his tone. 'I don't like the idea of fightin' those men. They have no part in this quarrel.'

'Then what can we do?'

'I figure we should get as many of the men together as we can and head back for town right away. If we can meet 'em on the trail, we might be able to take 'em by surprise.'

She studied him with a good deal of care for a moment, then gave a quick nod. 'I'll get them all together,' she murmured.

Chuck Houston stepped down off the boardwalk and made his way slowly over to the saloon. There was a lump on the back of his head as large as a pigeon's egg and he was in a bad humour. Weston's death had scarcely affected him. The other had been useful only so long as he had men and was willing to fight. But with Slade having escaped, he realized that he would have to do something drastic and fast, if he was to retain his position. He was still marshal here and he had sent a couple of men out to bring in the members of the Council. If they refused to do as he asked, then he would make things so hot for them they would be glad to co-operate with him.

There were seven of Weston's crew in the saloon, ranged along the bar, their backs to him as he entered. Thrusting his way forward, he held up a finger to the barkeep, downed the whiskey in a single gulp when it was poured for him, then filled his glass again from the bottle.

'Slade will ride hell for leather to the Lazy Y,' he said loudly, not looking round at the others. 'Then he'll come hightailin' it back to town, ready to burn the place. If any of you men have ideas of runnin' out now, then you'd better forget 'em.'

'Weston's dead,' snarled one of the men, a black-bearded man who towered head and shoulders above the others. 'We take orders from nobody now. Seems to me that you've been shootin' off your mouth a lot as to what you'd do with Slade when you got your hands on him. You didn't want him killed, you wanted him brung in alive so you could watch him die. If we'd shot him back there on the trail when we had him, none of this would've happened.'

'All right, so I made a mistake But we can still redeem ourselves. I've got men bringing the Council members over to the saloon. They'll be here in a couple of minutes. Then I'll get as many men for a posse as I need and when Slade and his men do get here, they'll get a warmer reception than they've bargained for.'

'How'd you know that the townsfolk will back you in this, Houston?' demanded another of the men further along the bar. 'Seems to me that you've been relyin' on us to do your dirty work for you. Don't recollect you gettin' anybody else to do it.'

Houston grimaced a little. 'They'd better back me up, or they'll have their town burned down about their ears. It won't be difficult to persuade 'em that this is why Slade is ridin' back into town. Men will do a lot to defend their homes and families, even fight with a marshal they don't like.'

'I say that it's still none of our business,' growled the black-bearded man harshly. 'We got no call to help you, or the town. We lost plenty of good men when we tried to destroy the Lazy Y. Now Weston is lyin' in the mortuary and we might follow him. That *hombre* Slade is a devil with a gun. And you heard what he said about havin' been sent here by the Governor. If we do kill him, could be they'll send troops next. I don't want to tangle with them.'

'You yeller, or somethin'?' grated Houston. 'I say you back me to the hilt now. You're all in this as deep as I am.

146

If one of us goes down, he takes the others with him. Don't forget that.'

'I'm forgettin' nothin'.' The other moved a step away from the counter. The reason behind the move was obvious, so that he had a clear sweep for his guns. 'But I'm headin' for the border and if you try to stop me, I'll kill you, Houston. Any of you others with guts and sense will follow me.'

Houston moved sideways a couple of paces, his eyes not leaving the other's face. He stood gently sprung at the knees in the typical gunman's stance, his gun arm cocked for the blurring downward sweep as soon as the other made his move.

The tall man stared back at him. There was no look of fear or cowardice in his face, but he seemed to have lost something in that single moment when Houston had moved away from the counter. His lips were parted, no longer drawn now into a thin, harsh line.

'You're makin' a mistake buckin' me like this, Marshal,' said the other after a brief pause. 'You're not facin' up to one of your townsfolk now, you know.'

'You gettin' set to talk me to death,' said Houston tautly. He was aware that the atmosphere now inside the saloon had grown suddenly electric, tensed. It was possible for him to see the other's face quite clearly, etched a little with shadow in the light of the lamps on the bar. He watched for the sudden fractional tightening of his lower lip, the sure sign that the other was ready to make his move.

'Make your play then, Marshal,' gritted the other.

Houston smiled faintly. 'I'm waitin' for you,' he said and there was something insolent and taunting about his tone.

A second went by, perhaps the space of a single heartbeat, but with all of eternity crowded into it. Then the other went for his gun. His shoulder dropped a little, his taloned fingers dipping for the butt of the gun in its

147

holster. His hand had moved with a blurring speed, striking downward like a rattler. Even as he moved, Houston whirled sideways, drew his gun and fired in the same instant.

The tall man's pistol exploded close on the heels of Houston's, but he had already been hit when he pressed the trigger, his body slammed backward by the leaden impact of the slug that struck him, ploughing into his chest, knocking him against the table at his back. The bullet tore up a sliver of wood out of the floor a couple of feet from where the marshal stood, the smoking gun still levelled on the other. The wounded man forced himself around with a tremendous effort, one hand pressed flat on the table as he strove to send strength into his buckling legs. His torn chest heaved as he tried to pull air down into his torn lungs, but already his eyes were glazing and there was a bubbling patch of blood beneath his shirt. He dropped his gun; folded at the knees, and crashed forward, one of the chairs splintering under his ponderous bulk as he fell on it.

Turning slowly, Houston faced the other men ranged along the bar. His voice was like ice, cold and brittle as he said: 'Anybody else want to argue the matter?'

There were no answers. One by one, the men turned their backs on the man slumped across the chair and finished their drinks. Houston waited for a few moments watching them with a speculative concentration, then he holstered the gun and went back to his own drink.

Five minutes later, the doors of the saloon opened and three men came in. Wallis the banker, led them. He looked nervous, as did his companions, and Houston saw him start as he glimpsed the body lying on the floor near the table. The reek of gunsmoke in the saloon was enough to tell these men that violent death had visited the place only a little while before.

'Well, gentlemen,' Houston said loudly. 'I'm glad that

you accepted my invitation. Bartender, pour my friends a drink. We have a lot to talk over.'

'Really, Marshal! I fail to see what we have to discuss,' said Thoroton, one of the storekeepers. 'If it is anything to do with the law and its being carried out, then it's up to you, not us. We did our job when we elected you to the post.'

'I know all that,' nodded the other. He let his keen gaze sweep from one man to the other, saw with satisfaction the way they lowered their glances as he looked at them. There would be very little difficulty here, he reflected. 'I want to warn you that my prisoner, Frank Slade, the man who shot down my brother in cold blood and who only recently broke out of the jail, shot Cal Weston and two of his men and also stole a horse, will be ridin' back into town with the Lazy Y crew at any minute. I don't think I need to remind you of the number of times that Ed Curry swore to fire the town if we didn't fall in with his wishes. Now that this killer, Slade, seems to have taken over command there, I doubt if there will be any change in that attitude.'

He saw the looks of consternation on their faces. 'But what can we do, Marshal?' queried Bailey in a quaking tone. 'None of us are gunfighters and we can't hope to stand up against the men of the Lazy Y.'

'I've got some men here with me,' Houston said easily. He nodded towards the men at the bar. 'They're all Cal Weston's men and they just want a chance to avenge his death. But I don't have enough men. I want to swear in a posse, deputise men who are willin' to fight to defend their homes. I don't suppose you have any notion of what happens when a bunch of cattlemen decide to ride in on a town and fire it. Believe me, it isn't nice.'

'We don't have the authority to force men to be deputised, Marshal,' said Wallis.

'Mebbe not, but a word from you gentlemen may make

any – reluctant – citizens see where their duty lies. That's all I'm askin' of you. Give me a chance to defend Cross Buttes.'

Wallis nodded after a brief pause. Inwardly, he knew that he had no choice in the matter. That Houston had already shot one man who had stood in his way, and he did not wish to go the same way himself. There was no telling how far Houston would go in his fight with Slade and the Lazy Y. At the back of his mind, he was not at all sure that Houston was right. There had been no trouble at all from the Lazy Y until this man had ridden into town and taken the post of Town Marshal. And when he came to think back on events at that time, it came to him that there had also been something strange about the way in which the old sheriff had died. They had never managed to catch the man who had bushwhacked him, shot him in the back, and although Houston had promised that he would do everything in his power to bring the killer to justice, nothing whatsoever had been done. The matter had been allowed to lapse and the killing was all but forgotten now. But sitting there, at the table in the saloon, staring across at Houston, it came to him that the other probably knew more about it than anyone else, that it could even have been him who had fired the killing shot. Certainly it seemed very fortunate that the sheriff had died in such circumstances, so that Houston might step in and take over. Once he had set himself up as the law in Cross Buttes, the way would be open for him and his brother to take over the town and then the surrounding territory.

But he wisely kept these thoughts to himself at that moment. To have spoken them out aloud would have been both foolish and possibly suicidal. But he kept them in his mind during the next hour, as he went around the town, arousing men from their beds, warning them that Slade was riding into town at that very moment, ready to brace the town.

The night passed slowly as the men began to gather.

From the door of the saloon, Houston watched them with a feeling of satisfaction. He was still in the game and with an excellent chance. It would be strange if this bunch of men could not wipe out Slade and his crew without too much trouble. He was not worried about the fact that several of the townsfolk would be killed themselves. In fact, that rather suited his purpose. It meant that there was a good chance that some of those who had been questioning his authority and speaking against him, might be wiped out, smoothing his path once this was all over. There would be the girl to handle too and that would have to be done with diplomacy, but he would be able to do that too once Slade was out of the way. Without him, and with the foreman, McCorg, possibly dead too, she would have nobody to turn to for help, would be forced to sell out to him at a low price.

Three miles out of town, Slade reined up his mount, held up his right hand to halt the column that rode with him. The brush whispered softly all about them, leaves rustling in the cold night air. There was the strong smell of sage in their nostrils, a sure sign of impending rain. The breeze itself was fitful, rustling one minute and then tingling his nerves, making him believe he heard hoofbeats in it, dying away completely the next. It was an eerie sound, but whenever he strained his ears to listen, it was only his imagination.

'You reckon they'll be headed out this way?' asked Forbes tensely. 'We're not far out of town and there's no sign of 'em yet.'

'I know. That's what worries me.' Slade ran a finger down his cheek. 'That last time they hit the ranch, they must've left town after we did, yet they probably got within sight of the ranch as soon as we arrived. There has to be another trail over the hills yonder.'

'There's an old Indian track there, but a man would be a fool to try to use it, especially in the dark. Too many slides along it for safety and one wrong step would send you down a two-hundred foot drop on to the rocks.'

'But they must have taken it on that other occasion,' Slade pointed out, 'and if they did the same tonight, we could've missed 'em in the darkness. That means the ranch will be undefended if they have given us the slip.'

The rest of the men stared at him in a silence that was full of obvious apprehension. The implications of what he had said, had sunk in at once. For a moment, Slade was on the point of ordering them to turn back, but he thrust the thought away. Their only chance lay in riding on into Cross Buttes and forcing the issue. Even if they turned now and rode hell for leather back to the ranch, they could not reach it in time. Still sorely troubled, he motioned the men forward.

They sighted Cross Buttes after a short, sharp ride, while it was still starlit darkness. Among the rocks, they paused, staring down at the cluster of dark buildings, with the white-dusty line of the main street splitting them in twain. There were a handful of lights showing, even at that hour of the morning and Slade eyed them with a faint feeling of apprehension. There was an air of watchful expectancy about the town which he did not like. It reminded him too forcibly of other towns such as this which he had known in the past, towns that stood on the brink of a gunfight which would tear the night apart in a splashing of muzzle fire and a screeching hail of bullets.

'What do you think, Frank?' asked Forbes softly.

'It's too damned quiet. They're in there all right and they'll be waitin' for us.'

'You want one of us to ride in and scout the place?'

Slade considered that for a moment, then shook his head. 'They'll be watchin' every trail into town,' he murmured. 'Reckon we'd better just ride in and accommodate 'em.'

Slowly, walking their horses, they rode towards the edge of town, eyes alert for any sudden suspicious movement, but they reached the end of the main street with the houses and store fronts standing quiet and dark on either side. The plankwalks seemed empty, but there was that familiar itch between Slade's shoulder blades and he knew the town was not as empty as it looked, that there were eyes watching their every move.

Halfway along the street, he paused at a sudden movement at the far end. Narrowing his eyes, he saw the line of men moving slowly towards them out of the shimmering starlit darkness that hung over the town and squeezed its velvet fingers around the buildings.

'Looks like company,' murmured Forbes tautly.

Slade nodded, pushed his sight through the darkness, sucking in his breath as his gaze rested on the line of figures moving at a snail's pace in their direction. He could see no sign of Houston there, guessed that the other would be hiding somewhere in the background, waiting for these men to do his dirty work for him; and that made the marshal doubly dangerous. He was the sort of snake who would fire from cover and without any warning, would shoot a man in the back and claim he had fired in self defence.

'Where's Houston,' said Forbes through lips stretched tight over his teeth.

'Keep your eyes open for that murderin' coyote,' Slade said. 'He's somewhere around, waitin' for a chance to spot us before we see him. Watch the upstairs windows. He could be anywhere there with a rifle.'

He halted his mount, stood with legs thrust straight and deep into the stirrups. The line of men halted when they were less than fifty feet away, standing quite still like one man. Most of them carried rifles or wore handguns. Slade recognized one or two of them as storekeepers, men who had no part in this fight.

He called loudly. 'We've got no quarrel with any of you men. This is something between us and Houston. If any of Weston's men are still around and want to back up that crooked marshal they're welcome to do so, but we don't want to shoot down innocent men.'

There was an awkward pause, then one of the men yelled harshly: 'We know all about you, Slade. You're followin' Curry's orders. Even though he's dead you want to burn the town. Well, we're here to stop you. We know what happens when trailmen move in to brace a town. That ain't goin' to happen here. We're ready to defend our homes.'

Slade felt a sudden shock of surprise. Then this was how Houston had got these men on his side, warning them that the Lazy Y men were riding in to burn the town. Swiftly, he retorted: 'That's just a pack of lies that Houston has told you to get you to back him. If he's supposed to be the law in this town, where is he? Skulking someplace in the darkness, leavin' you to face us while he saves his own skin.'

There was some subdued muttering among the line of men at that remark, and Slade saw that one or two were beginning to doubt what Houston had told them. He tried to press home .his advantage. 'Get Houston to step out here and make those charges to our faces,' he said. 'He's just waitin' until you've been shot down and then he'll have strengthened his position. I'm here to clean this territory up on the Governor's orders. Houston is a wanted killer. There are half a dozen sheriffs lookin' for him right now. They reckoned he'd ridden south of the Texas border into Mexico, but he's been hidin' here all the time. Wouldn't surprise me none if he wasn't the man who killed your last sheriff.'

'We've got no proof you're a marshal,' said one of the men harshly. 'Could be you're just tryin' to squirm out of this.'

'You're wrong. I'm here to see that Houston is brought to justice.'

'Then where is your badge, mister?' shouted another man. He held a rifle in the crook of his elbow. Glancing down, Slade recognized one of the men who had ridden with Weston. So Houston had planted some of these men with the crowd. It seemed he had no answer to this, that there would be bloodshed here in the main street which he could not avoid.

Then, abruptly, a voice called from the boardwalk to the rear of the men. 'He's tellin' the truth. I helped him escape from the jail after I'd sent a telegram to the Governor. Frank Slade is workin' for him.'

Slade turned in the direction of the voice, saw the tall, thin figure of the doctor standing on top of the wooden steps. The other went on hurriedly: 'Houston has tricked all of you.'

'Why you—' began the man in the front rank. He swung swiftly, bringing his rifle to bear on the doctor.

Before he could complete his turn, Slade's hand moved with lightning speed. The long-barrelled Colt in his fist roared once, the crimson lick of flame spearing into the darkness. The man uttered a low grunt, clutched at his chest, the rifle clattering at his feet as he staggered back, blundered into the man next to him, then dropped to his knees in the dust.

In front of him, the rest of the men stood hesitantly, still unsure of themselves at this sudden turn of events. Then they lowered their guns and moved aside. Slade nodded, let his pent-up breath go through his lips, gigged his mount forward, knowing there would be no trouble from these men. Behind him, the other riders followed, making their way forward slowly, searching the dark shadows on either side.

They had almost reached the end of the street and still there had been no sign of Chuck Houston and the other men he had with him. Slade debated whether the other had left the town, running out while his luck still held. It was possible that Houston had foreseen this eventuality, had been waiting close to the southern outskirts of the town where he could see how things progressed and when he had heard only that one shot, he would have known that things had gone against him, that his only hope lay in flight.

Then there came a sudden cry from a doorway on their right: 'Slade! Watch out from the saloon.'

Slade whirled swiftly, instinctively in the saddle. The other saloon in Cross Buttes, situated at the southern end of the main street, was in almost total darkness, but his eyes caught the sudden movement at once. The faint starlight glinted off the metal barrel of a rifle in one of the upstairs windows. Even as the other fired, Slade's gun had roared twice. The swiftness with which he had opened up on the assassin, coupled with the man's warning cry from the street had put the other off his shot. He had hurried it, pressed the trigger before he was really ready. The bullet hit the horse instead of Slade. The bay reared wildly, threshing with its legs and it was all that Slade could do to fight it down. Then he dropped swiftly from the saddle, slapped the animal on the rump, sending it galloping along the street while he ran for the saloon.

The move had taken the hidden marksman by surprise. Inevitably, his gaze had followed the swiftly running horse and his second shot, loosed off swiftly, ploughed into the dirt several feet behind Slade's hurtling body as he dropped undercover at the edge of the boardwalk near the door of the saloon. Scrambling to his feet, Slade raced for the entrance, ran inside without pausing. In the darkness, he cast about him, saw the wide stairs which led to the upper floor in the dimness at the far end of the long bar.

He paused for a moment, trying to guess at Houston's intentions. The other was still upstairs, and unless he tried to get out around the veranda high above the street and risk being shot by the men waiting in the road, he would have to come down by the stairs. Therefore Slade continued on until he reached the end of the bar, working his way forward along the front of it, keeping his head down. Halting, he listened intently. He could hear no sound from

156

the top of the stairs, waited for a second and then began to work his way up them, feeling forward with one hand outstretched in front of him. Halfway up, he heard the faint sound. It seemed to come from one of the rooms along the short and narrow passage at the very top of the stairs. The sound of a man easing his way around a door which would have creaked ominously if he had opened it any further.

Sucking in a heavy gust of air, he let it come out through his nostrils in short, slow pinches of sound. He remained rigid for a long moment, seeing nothing, in the darkness, trying to estimate where the other was just by the sounds he was making. There was a sharp rattle of metal striking wood, the sound that the butt of a Winchester would make if it caught the edge of a half open door.

For a long second after that, there was absolute silence in the building. It was so quiet that Slade could hear the pounding of his own heart m his chest.

Nothing came from outside, although he knew the rest of the men would have worked their way all around the building now, so that there was no escape for Chuck Houston.

The silence stretched out long and it was Houston who broke first. He let his wind go in a harsh gasp, then said loudly: 'I know you're there, Slade. If you reckon you've got the guts to come up and take me, then what are you waitin' for?'

The vast emptiness of the building diffused his voice and the echoes that rattled from one side to the other, made it difficult to tell just where Houston was. Slade edged to the very side of the stairs, pressing his body down to present a more difficult target if the other opened up, firing wildly into the darkness. He heard the marshal's body move again, the sudden sound betraying the man's uneasiness. He heard the boards of the corridor creak as he stepped forward, testing them with his weight.

'Why the hell don't you step out and face me?' called the other thinly. 'I know you're out there.'

From somewhere ahead of him, Slade heard the other's breathing, hurried and shallow, the sounds a nervous man made when he was afraid. Lifting his arm slowly, he aimed his gun into the almost pitch blackness where he judged the other to be and squeezed the trigger. The bright glare of the muzzle flash, a blue-crimson bloom of light in the darkness, lit the top of the stairs. The thunderous sound of the explosion was a tremendous noise in that confined space, cracking on Slade's ears. He heard the bullet strike something hard and metallic, go shrieking off in murderous ricochet along the passage. The sound was followed almost at once by a sharp yell of pain from the other and the unmistakable clatter of a heavy weapon falling to the floor. There was no immediate return of fire from the other and it came to Slade that he had somehow hit the barrel of Houston's rifle, knocking it from his grasp. He could hear the man fumbling with his six gun, jerking it from its holster, and fired again, shifting his aim slightly.

Muzzle light leapt back at him from the darkness. He felt the wind of a bullet close to his cheek, ducked instinctively. In the brief flash, he saw Houston standing there, saw him rush forward and jerked up his gun, firing a single shot. In the heart of the racket, he heard the man give up a loud, terrible cry. Then the other had gone blundering past him, falling against the wooden rail that ran along the edge of the upper floor. For a second, Slade had the impression of the other lying there, halfway over the rail, a dark shadow, half seen. Then there came the splintering of wood, cracking under the other's weight. Rising to his feet, he moved forward, but before he could even reach the man, he had fallen out into the darkness as the rail collapsed beneath him, hurling him forward.

Breathing heavily, he thrust the Colt back into leather, walked slowly down the stairs. He was almost at the bottom when he heard somebody come into the saloon and a moment later, there was the brief flare of a match as one

158

of the men lit a lamp, holding it high over his head, look-ing about him in the yellow light.

Forbes came over to where Slade stood at the bottom of the stairs. He said tersely: 'What happened, Frank?'

'He's dead.' Slade pointed. 'Fell from the rail up there.'

Houston lay on his back amid the smashed remains of one of the tables. His eyes were open, wide and staring, looking at them as the yellow pool of light from the lantern fell on him. But the eyes saw nothing. There was a spreading red stain on the front of his shirt, discolouring the badge he had pinned to it.

Acting on a sudden impulse, Forbes bent, hooked his strong fingers around the edges of the badge and pulled hard. The fabric of the shirt tore as he yanked the badge off, stared at it for a moment, then slipped it into his pocket.

'Reckon we can save that until we find a man worthy to wear it,' he said succinctly.

They went out into the street, quiet now, with little knots of men standing in the shadows. Wallis, the banker, came forward. He said hesitantly: 'I guess we owe you an apology, Mister Slade. Seems we were wrong all the way as far as Houston was concerned.'

'He's dead now,' Slade said wearily. 'I suggest that you get yourselves a straight-shootin' lawman and back him to the hilt. My work here is finished now that Houston is dead.'

Turning on his heel, he walked back to where one of the men was holding his mount, swung up stiffly into the saddle. The rest of the men formed up behind him and they rode slowly out of Cross Buttes, cutting north. Already, the moon had set and towards the east, the stars which had been so bright during the night were beginning to dim. The sage still smelled as strongly as before, promis-ing rain, but as yet, the sky was perfectly clear and cloud-less and there was a faint bar of silver lying over the hori-zon to the east, silhouetting the rising curves of the hills.

It was full daylight when they rode down the grassy

slopes into the courtyard of the Lazy Y. Slade swung down from the saddle, turned the horse loose into the corral and then made his way towards the house. She was there waiting for him. At the sight of him, she got up from the high-backed chair on the porch and came to the very edge of the veranda, stood looking down at him for a long moment, a look of immense thankfulness on her face.

'Are you all right, Frank?' she asked in a low tone.

He nodded, took her hand and led her back to the chair. 'Everything is all right now,' he said. 'It's finished. I don't think there will be any more trouble in Cross Buttes.'

'I thought you would never come back,' she said softly, looking down at her intertwined fingers in her lap. Then she glanced up. 'I'll make us some coffee. You look as though you could use some.'

He nodded in agreement, even then she made no immediate move to rise. When she did get up, she stood very close to him and he smelled the faint perfume on her hair.

'Do you have to leave us now?' she asked in a very small voice. 'If you ride out now I don't know how I will be able to manage this place, with McCorg so badly hurt. I – I want you to stay here, Frank.'

She did not move away as he caught her arms, nor when he drew her to him. He looked down at her face and saw there, all the things he had wanted to see, things he had never thought to see. She was smiling up at him now, holding him tightly.

'I guess I might be able to get the Governor to do without me from now on,' he said gently. 'These hills, these valleys, are good. Only some of the men who live here are bad.'

'Everything can be made good if only we have the faith and the will to try,' she told him. The pressure of her hands drew his head down to her and they stood there, oblivious of the heavy drops of rain which suddenly began to fall from the cool, overcast heavens.